TROLLS

J.J.M. CZEP

Brick Cave Media
brickcavebooks.com
2014

Brick Cave Media
brickcavebooks.com
2014

DEDICATION

To all the children who have been a part of my life, and those who someday may be, I am consistently in awe of how much you have taught me. Youth is an adventure that ends too soon. Breathe in every moment!

To the writers, family, and friends who continue to help me grow, thank you for your patience, and persistence.

And, to the cruel people and scary things, you inspire me, too. To create balance there must be monsters.

ACKNOWLEDGEMENTS

So much thanks to Sharon Skinner for helping to make this edition of Trolls the very best, and for all the smiley faces when I needed to be reminded that, even though I have much to learn, there are good things in there, too.

A huge thank you to Sarah Price, whose cover art for this story truly brought me to tears of joy when I first saw it.

Thank you to Bob Nelson and everyone at Brick Cave Media for giving me a chance to get this story out there to an even bigger audience.

Thank you to all the people who saw the potential in the rough drafts! Look! Now, it's shiny!

TROLLS

J.J.M. CZEP

Brick
Cave Media

Brick Cave Media
brickcavebooks.com
2014

CHAPTER ONE:
THE TROLL, THE DANGERS OF THE JUNGLE, AND THE BRIDGE

Thump, scratch, scratch. Thump, scratch, scratch.

The troll's fearsome footsteps ascended the mountain slope. The creature approached my tiny cabin.

Gathering the corners of the tablecloth, I rounded the table set for chess. The chipped and cracked game pieces clattered against one another, improving character with every ping. No time to wonder if the troll heard the din, I shushed as if the miniature army could hear me. I rolled the bundle beneath the bed and clattered the table onto its side.

The footfalls paused outside. The troll had most certainly heard. I sat frozen, back against the bottom of the table. The troll jostled the door handle. My eyes ran mad about the room. In sudden inspiration I righted the table, threw myself onto the bed and hid behind a book.

The door cried on its hinges, signaling the troll's entry.

I dared not look.

Its breathing labored from the trek. It rasped toward me. I stayed behind my book, my breathing equally ragged from my run around the room.

"Emily Marie." The troll leaned close.

I tipped the book just enough to make eye contact and coated my voice with sugar. "Yes Auntie?"

Pale blue eyes burned like twin lamps. "What have you been doing all this time? Up to trouble, no doubt." Auntie always saw through my best efforts to act innocent.

"Reading, Auntie, only reading." I offered my shield.

Auntie shuffled farther into my tiny sanctuary, her cane scraping the floor every other step. Grateful for the acres of overstuffed and over-frilled pillows, I sank below the edges of my open book into soft and scratchy folds.

I averted my gaze to the image on the page and met eyes as cold as Auntie's. The caption at the top read, "TROLL."

A bit too quick and a bit too loud, I shut the monster inside the book.

"Is it time for my lessons? I can think of no other reason you would trouble your dear self to climb all the way up the stairs." Without awaiting answer, I leapt from my bed and bolted for the door. A flourish of frills marked my exit.

Auntie called after, inquiring about something under the bed. She had discovered my army bundled in cloth. I felt secure that she could never bend low enough to capture them, so left Auntie, the Troll, to wonder all she wished. No matter how unladylike Auntie thought the set, it was a gift from mother I would not give up.

The landing at the top of the stairs served as a place to check if the troops stalled Auntie from looking down the main hallway. Assured they had, I swung one pale leg over the banister, my pink bloomers flashing the entryway below. One last check to be sure. No witnesses. A good shove and down I shot. I reveled a moment, soft curls dancing about my ears. Rear first, down the orange-scented, polished rail, I glided. A reverse somersault off the curve of the banister landed the dismount. I vaulted to my feet and bowed to the copper and crimson autumn entryway banners, then marched to the solarium for my lessons.

Sun glittered through blue-green windows in the small and always warm room. Auntie insisted on calling the tiny room, with only space for a school desk, a rocking chair and a tangle of plant life a solarium. I insisted on calling it the Jungle.

Unlike children in the village, I did not have a weekday morning send-off to school. My lessons took place in the Jungle under the watchful tutelage of the Princess. Auntie was certain I would learn more than academics in the public school system. Factories for production of delinquents, the reason for society's downfall, she called them. I did not understand such things, but the way I saw it, anything Auntie hated was bound to be a ton of fun.

On days when temperamental clouds imprisoned the sun, or at night when leafy shadows played cruel games of hide and seek, there was no scarier place than the Jungle. Today, it was magical. No shadows, only glittering sunlit glass. The sort of day that made me love the Jungle. Freshly watered plants burned green with life. I waded happily, lazily, in puddles of fragrance, dripping invisible pools in the air surrounding each bloom. Even this late in fall the Jungle hoarded spring.

"Good morning, Emily dear." Pale pink lips smiled beneath the greenest buds in the Jungle.

I smiled a wistful greeting in return. It always took a moment to remember how to speak upon seeing the Princess of the Jungle.

"'Morning, Mother," I breathed, shaking my head clear of the magic of the flowers.

Mother's beauty, stunning in any room, was nowhere more awe inspiring than in the solarium. She slid into her white wicker throne and set a large book across her slender lap. Under her spell I floated to my seat, but crashed upon reading the title on the workbook, ARITHMETIC. The Jungle had many dangers, but this was its most fearsome beast. I slumped in my chair, the room suddenly too warm for thinking.

As I calculated the strange mathematical equations concerning trains and cities, apples and oranges, my pencil practiced her paper ballet. She glided around smooth figure eights, and executed perfect tens, her slim yellow figure twisting in my fingertips. I gazed, entranced by sunlight glinting off her beautiful silver necklace and graceful one-footed leaps and turns. How smooth her transitions from one number to the next. If only she could be allowed more often to dance freely to the music in my mind. Instead, she and I were always bound to the choreography of charts and graphs of arithmetic. I wondered what we might create if given a page as endlessly outstretched as my imaginings. How big could drawing pages be made, I mused.

"Emily." Mother's voice caused the ballerina to trip and break her shoe. "Emily, it is lesson time, not day dream time," she chided.

"Hmmm?" I studied the tip of the pencil jutting at an odd angle.

"Dear Emily." Mother sighed.

I stared blankly at her, past the broken pencil point, still between worlds.

She rose from her throne and slipped the wounded dancer from my grasp. I loved the Princess and her Jungle, but despaired at being trapped. I laid my head, heavy with too much information, upon the open workbook. I turned my head to gaze out over the gray-green moor. I envisioned my self, frolicking through patches of dandelions. The day was far too nice for lessons, especially arithmetic. Mother set the newly sharpened pencil at the tips of my fingers. I gazed over it, making it part of the scenery—a bridge, a walkway, a sulfur-hued river. Mother's eyes set over the bridge, resting at the horizon.

"Emily, dear." Mother set her palms on the edge of the desk and rested her chin upon them.

I stared blankly into the green moons before me.

"You have one hour. The clock is ticking. Now, go play." Eyes smiling, she stood and petted my curls into place.

It took no more than a moment for the offer to sink in before I was off. One hour. I rejoiced! A truly generous amount when considering the wrath the Princess of the Jungle might incur from the Troll for my momentary freedom. I would remember this gracious gift and honor the Princess. Cookies, perhaps.

Stepping off the back porch with a leap from the creaking boards, I burst into the glow of the early afternoon sun and shivered. The view from the Jungle fooled me once again. While all inside the glass walls remained warm year-round outside, chill winds rolled along, riding shallow valleys.

Refusing to waste precious time, and risk the possibility of running into Auntie by going back for warmer clothing, I stretched my knee socks to my thighs and pulled my bloomers to meet them, covering my legs from the biting breeze. I wasn't heading into the Arctic this time, I reasoned. I jumped about and pumped my arms and legs. Being silly made one warm. The embarrassment of being caught at the very least warmed the cheeks.

No time to spend on silliness though. Today, I had a mission. The acres that made up the manor grounds were far greater than what Auntie and Mother could afford to maintain. The gardener—a nice gentleman from town, according to Mother; a foolish young cad, if you asked Auntie—made certain the front of the house and a nice reasonable yard remained well groomed. I am sure he would've done much more if only Mother had asked, but I am only eight, what would I know about such adult matters. I had often used my recess between lessons, those not chaperoned by Auntie anyway, to explore beyond the groomed portion of the rear yard.

At one time, the gazebo just beyond the outside entrance of the Jungle had been quite a sight. I recalled photographs of its glory. It now depended on the overgrown ivy and shrubbery to hold the sagging roof up. One visit to the gazebo led to the discovery that the briared bushes had once been a manicured, heart-shaped ring of roses. This once tribute to the Goddess of Love was now the remains of the numerous family weddings I had seen pictures of.

I paid my respects with an offering of water from a rusted coffee can and promised to steal a pair of Mother's oven mitts to pull away the strangling weeds. I had high hopes for a blooming garden by June. Visions of red roses surrounding and climbing the alabaster pillars of my temple to Venus warmed my mind as I ventured past on to the ruins.

I hoped it would not take more than an hour to explore my latest discovery. It was always depressing to stop in the middle of a really good find. I had already been torn away more than once.

I followed the river for several days in search of civilization till I finally came upon what looked to be an ancient bridge. Its stones crumbled in places, but it appeared, for the most part, stable. Mosses and ivy overtook the stone rails. A pair of pale brick sentinels stood guard at either side of the crossing. The pillars crumbled beneath the weight of large stone orbs resting upon them.

Keeping a cautious eye out for trolls, I approached the structure. In this part of the world, trolls often guarded bridges such as this. The ghoulish creatures, particularly fond of human flesh, feared light and thus remained beneath the bridges they guarded. They are tricky, and if they can get a traveler to look over the edge of the rails, even for a moment, they reach their great arms out and drag the unsuspecting victim down.

I edged onto the walkway. It seemed stable

enough as I crept a bit further toward the center and offended the bricks with a small jump. Nothing fell away. I grinned and gauged the distance with a spit, then bent like a sprinter. With fingers splayed on the coarse cobbling. I crouched and counted to three. The imagined starting pistol echoed through my mind as I darted across.

I took the length of the crossing in a handful of strides, but a noise from behind took the wind from my victory. The fearless adventurer in me melted. I watched in horror as a hole opened in the center of the stone structure. The hole expanded before my eyes. Panic ran through my legs as I scurried up and down the river's edge. There had to be a way back to the other side. The water was not that deep. I considered wading across, though this late in fall the water would be terribly cold. Not to mention, there was no telling what lurked below the mud and murk. Auntie would skin me alive if I came home with stockings and dress stained with muck.

I stared at the crumbled center of the bridge. Perhaps I could jump across. The remaining bits of bridge might yet be stable. I jumped on the edge. No crumbling. To get a better idea of the distance, I sidled along the rail toward the gap. It yawned bigger than Auntie's scolding mouth. Leaping such a distance would be tricky, if possible. Even if I did make it, there was no telling how stable the edges were on the other side.

I stared over the railing. Trolls or no trolls, I had to get across this bridge.

I swung one leg over the rail and froze. To think this was a good idea bordered on insanity. I would have more than a muddied dress to worry about if I fell. I started out crawling along the narrow rail. The water chuckled as the bridge snagged my dress pulling me off balance. Walking the rail had seemed easier in my head.

Careful to avoid mossy patches, I sidled along the slippery rail. My left foot passed the opposite edge of the hole when the wind betrayed me. It caught my skirt and everything went terribly wrong. The world tipped, but there was nothing I could do to stop my keeling. My feet lost the struggle to regain a grip on the rail and I fell.

CHAPTER TWO:
UNDER THE BRIDGE, OVER THE BRIDGE, AND
INTO MY DREAMS

I awoke to voices. At first I thought Auntie and Mother had found me and taken me back to the house. These voices, three in all, were younger, though. They seemed to come from everywhere at once, but I could not see the speakers.

"So, what are we," a squeaking voice

"Going to do with her?" followed by another's.

"Sir?" asked in unison.

"I don't know!" a boyish voice cut the air, "I have to think."

"We thought—"

"this bridge—"

"was abandoned!"

"A practice bridge." The two small voices tossed the sentence, chorusing the last part.

"What is a practice bridge?" I rolled to see where they came from.

In the murky dark I made out an array of knick-knacks and broken toys shelved within high walls of rock. I was surrounded. The floor squished beneath my elbows and knees as I moved on the spongy carpet. The ooze and stench of mud accompanied each movement as I moved into a crouch. I feared standing up, since I could not see the ceiling. On hands and knees I felt my way toward the voices.

The sticky mud clung to my dress. Auntie would be furious.

"Halt, intruder!" I still could not see anyone, but I made note of the very shiny, very pointy object directed at my nose.

I backed away so I wasn't seeing the blade in double. One was quite enough. Unfortunately, I backed too much and upset something behind me. Sending up a spray of muck, I spun. Three gruesome faces grinned, vacant eyes staring at me.

Trolls!

I was held captive by trolls. They had pulled me into the river. They would tear my flesh and drink my blood and chew my knuckles like bubble gum. I had to escape.

A light illuminated the cave. "Ah-ha! Vile beasties!" I stood. "Someone has come for me!" The light gave me courage. "They brought a light to burn your flesh! Run foul creatures!"

"Stupid girl." A boy about my age stood before me. He turned up the lamp he held to light the full chamber.

"Those are not beasties . . ."

"Those are just . . ."

"Our masks." Words danced from the grinning lips of two young children.

The older boy brushed at his matted hair as he stepped past me. "I think you broke mine!"

11

He wore in what looked like trousers and a nightshirt and was caked from head to toe, in mud and leaves. His moss colored eyes caught mine and he scowled.

The young duo was dressed about the same. One with a large dirty rag tied around wild curly-cued hair in a sad bow. Otherwise the two were identical.

"You're not trolls." I crossed my arms over my chest and leaned away.

"Yes, we are." The boy pointed a short but very sharp sword in my face. "And you are an intruder in our home." His tone was fierce, but he stood barely my height. "How did you get here?"

I knocked the blade aside. "What do you mean calling yourselves trolls and playing with sharp objects?" I returned the glare. "I fell into the river and that is all I remember. If I ended up in your home, it was not my intention."

The boy puffed his chest and stood toe to toe with me. He stretched his neck a bit, in an effort to make himself taller than me. "We are trolls."

"Are trolls!" the smaller children sang out.

"Are trolls!" They danced around us.

I wasn't about to back down from this challenge. "Everyone knows trolls are hairy, smelly, gruesome beasts that eat children and fear the light." I pointed to the oil lamp he had set in the corner.

"Everyone knows," the boy countered, "trolls are infants and children claimed by the water and never heard from again. They scare stupid humans who dare cross their bridges, eat bugs and grubs and too much candy, and fear neither light nor darkness."

One of the smaller children pulled the boy's shirt

just then and whispered into his ear.

"Mostly, we don't fear darkness." He rolled his eyes. "So there, stupid know-it-all girl." He stuck out his tongue and the other two mirrored the act.

They had to be playing some sort of game. Though they did look like they lived under a bridge. I looked at the mask in the boy's hands and the pair leaning on the ground. They did resemble the pictures in my books.

"I was an infant dumped in a river." I thought this a very good point to add. "That was eight years ago, and I was fished out just fine." I had their attention, so I continued. "I mean it was a narrow river. Well, mostly a stream that ribboned across the edge of the land the manor is on, and it wasn't my real family that found me."

The boy glared a moment. The other two watched for some clue what to do next. I crossed my arms and waited. Let's see how well thought out this game really is.

The boy let his blade fall with a squish to the mossy floor. "You're the lost troll . . ."

The other two leeched onto my arms and began jumping about.

"You? A stupid girl is the lost troll that was supposed to have been in charge of this bridge?" As he questioned, he made the rudest faces. "No. No! I cannot, do not, believe it."

The smaller children kept on their dance with my arms. I was too confused to do anything.

I suddenly panicked. "What time is it?" I asked more forcefully than intended.

The twins stopped their dance and the boy's face contorted. I shook my head and looked about. I shrugged the twins off my arms and patted my dried clothes. I had been here more than an hour for sure. I searched the walls for and opening. I had to get home.

Auntie would skin me for sure! I thought about the punishments I would receive as I patted the walls and shoved toys askew.

"What are you looking for?" The boy threw out his arms.

"A way out." I no longer wanted to play this silly game. "I have to get home." Though part of me wanted to stay, no part of me wanted to anger Auntie. "Do you have the time? How long have I been down here?"

"You can't leave now." He crossed his arms. "You know our secrets."

I caught sight of the pouting faces of the twins.

"Besides . . ." He jutted a thumb to the ceiling. "That is the only way in or out."

Far above the scattering of toys, a quarter-sized point of light shone. I marched to a wall and, using the makeshift shelves as footholds, climbed up. I didn't care if they tried to stop me. I didn't care that the ragged stone tore my stockings and knees. All I cared about was getting out of this strange little prison.

"You'll never make it to the top," the boy shouted.

I kept my eyes on the ever-growing opening in the darkness. Of course, I would make it. If this was the only way out, it couldn't be that difficult. How did they get home every night? And if it was the only way in, well I had already come through the opening once. When I reached the top, I stuck my hand through to find something to grab on to. I pulled back immediately. It was cold and wet—as if I had just dipped into a pool of freezing water. I pushed up to see through the opening. The sun was still high, but the view was odd. The yellow glow seemed diffused, frosted, rippled, as if . . . as if I was looking up through water! I lost my footing and plummeted back to the mossy carpet with a loud squish.

"I told you you wouldn't make it." The boy's tone dripped with scorn.

The trio stared down at me.

"For your information, I did make it all the way to the top. It's just ... just ..." I blinked, trying to make sense of it.

"I told you. Once you are in, you are in." He set his hands on his hips.

I really could not take much more of his arrogance.

"No one is sure how the lost troll made it out the first time." He stuck the sword into the mucky floor. "If what you say about being left at the river is true."

The twins came into view again. They seemed so sad, but I would not let that hinder my goal.

"If there is no other way out than that opening, then that is how I will get out."

All three jumped back as I stood.

I mounted the walls once more, this time determined to succeed.

There was an explanation for the water problem. Auntie and Mother always said there was logic to everything. For the moment, I hoped they were right. I reached my hand through. It came back soaked again. I held my breath and dove—if that is the proper term—upwards.

I should be able to hold my breath long enough to reach the surface of the shallow river, I reasoned. The river fooled me again, though.

Certain my entire body was now in the water, I struggled for the surface. I despised opening my eyes under water, but I had to find out where I was. Still aimed straight up, the distance to the rippling sunlight remained unchanged. How could this be? I was at least four feet into the water.

My lungs began to ache. I had to take a breath soon. Hopefully, not too soon, else it would be fatal. I pushed at the water as hard as I could, arms and legs flailing. I wished I had taken swim lessons. With a final kick, I burst to surface and sucked in precious air. The warmth of clear sunlight touched my hair and skin.

How had the river be so deep? I was now standing in only waist deep water, no more than a foot from the bridge. I looked beneath the water, where I thought I had come from. I kicked at the mud and smooth rocks in the riverbed.

Nothing.

No grotto. No toys. No trolls.

I could see the bottom if I really tried.

I examined my clothing. Dress torn, stockings browned, completely soaked through and through. I was going to be in so much trouble. Auntie would claim a few good whacks with her wooden spoon for this. Not to mention how late I was getting back.

"My lessons!" I cursed at the bridge, the river, and the strange children and their little game. I ran back to the house as fast as my sopping clothes and shoes allowed. As I breezed past the glass walls of the Jungle, I glimpsed Mother reading peacefully.

Maybe, she had lost track of time.

I snuck past the bushes, so as not to be caught out of the corner of her eye. I squished up the backstairs to the kitchen. I hoped the sun would dry the marks before anyone caught wise. Maybe no one would notice muddy tracks up the back walk. I kicked off my shoes at the kitchen door and stuffed my stockings down the front of my dress as I peered into the small side window. I only hoped Auntie wasn't making dinner yet. The coast was clear. I dried my feet as best I could before tiptoeing onto the cold tile.

No time to check the time on the large grandfather clock in the dining room, I scurried up the staircase. My pruned feet squeaked on the polished wood down the hallway to my bedroom. Slipping to the door, I turned the knob and hurried to shut myself in.

Safe.

I tossed my soiled and soaking garments into the laundry chute. Something I rarely did without being asked. This time it was important. I hoped no one would notice the grimy pile until they were at least dry.

Even with a clean dress and stockings my body felt caked with dirt. Maybe Mother wouldn't notice. I hiked my stockings up as I ran out the door and slid along the hallway. I rounded the staircase and in one movement—I didn't even check if anyone was watching—lifted sidesaddle onto the banister and launched down. I was in the Jungle in less than a minute—panting.

I tried to compose myself as best I could before entering, but it was no good. All the excitement and the running made my breathing ragged. I practically fell into my seat.

"Emily?" Mother looked up from her book, some romance novel or other. "Emily, did you look at the time?"

The time! I had not even thought to check how much trouble I was in.

"You still have forty minutes of recess." She looked at the dainty watch on her wrist. "Are you so eager to get back to your lessons?"

"Forty minutes" I was gone only twenty minutes.

Impossible, it took that much time just to get to the bridge. Maybe I imagined the whole thing? I realized I was gazing at Mother.

She was still waiting for an answer.

"Yes!" I breathed out the word a bit too loud. "Yes. I couldn't wait to get back to you and my lessons." I smiled lovingly. I wondered if she could see the utter confusion in my eyes.

"Weren't you wearing a different dress before you left?" Mother closed her book and set it on her lap.

I looked down at my outfit then back at Mother and shrugged. She shook her head and sighed, but opened her copy of the textbook.

The remainder of the afternoon went on without excitement. Not that lessons were ever exciting. My racing thoughts did make it go by much faster, though.

The crumbling bridge, the sudden depth of the river, and the mysterious grotto all seemed so incredibly real and yet so completely impossible.

At five o'clock, Mother looked at her watch and sent me upstairs to wash for dinner. Typically, I would make a mess in my room until called back down at six. Tonight, I took a full bath. I lingered in the steamy, sudsy water, watching my toes at the opposite end of the tub. I washed my hair more times than I usually would in a week. It felt so good to be free of the itchy, smelly memory of my swim in the river.

What I could not wash away was the children's mocking voices. That boy had been worst of all. I decided long ago that boys were icky, vile animals. This boy served to reinforce my theory. Although, the smaller children seemed fun. I wondered if they played there every day, if they were real at all. Even if they were, I was not sure how to get back to their hidden clubhouse.

The idea of a lost troll kept playing at my mind. What was it about the little game of being trolls that struck such a chord?

My toes played with the cork chain a long time before finally releasing the water. I looked at my wrinkled hands. For the second time today I had pruned my skin. This time was much more pleasant.

I wrapped a plush white towel around my body and rolled my curls into a knot upon the top of my head. I smiled at the regal Roman Goddess reflected in the steamed and foggy glass. Trolls. I scoffed at the thought. How could such a lovely visage ever be called a troll? I made an ugly face and skipped across the hallway to my room.

I pulled on my third dress of the day. This time I chose the softest, most comfortable bloomers, dug through my stocking drawer and found a pair of good woolen knee-highs, I wanted to be as cozy as possible. I really wanted to put my nightgown on, but I knew Auntie would not allow pajamas to dinner. At least, it wasn't Sunday, so I could get away with house slippers, and I did.

I combed out my curls into a giant brunette cloud. I loved how the soft hair tickled my ears and the back of my neck. I tamed the thick curls with a headband. Auntie hated my wild child hair, though behind her back Mother said it gave my face character. I checked my appearance in the mirror on my door and sighed. I poked at the dark blue veils beneath my eyes. I really wasn't hungry. All I wanted was my bed and to forget all about this day.

I trudged down to the dining room. I didn't even bother sliding down the banister this time. Auntie and Mother could probably see from just off the entryway, and I barely had the energy to take each step. I savored the plush softness of the slippers as I dragged to table and slumped into my chair.

"Good evening, Emily." Mother smiled as she sat down across from me, setting the last serving dish in front of her.

"Don't slouch." Auntie already sat primly at the head of the table.

I smiled at the both of them and sat up as straight as I could. Barley soup. On most evenings, I would have turned my nose up at it and tried to make it look like I was eating. Tonight though, the more warmth I could get into me the better. The chill that still clung from the river finally shivered off with each spoonful and I sniffled back the stirrings of a cold.

Dinner was, as usual, eaten in near silence. Mother mentioned only once that being as tomorrow was Saturday, and the gardener would be here, I would have the day off from lessons. Auntie gave her a glare of disapproval. I never really understood why. Usually, I would dare an inquiry as to whether we should picnic near the temple to discuss my landscaping plans with the expert. This would lead to more sour looks from Auntie and Mother turning the color of roses. Tonight I was just too exhausted.

I poked at the potatoes, too hard and starchy to enjoy, and didn't even bother to tear into the boiled, rubbery stew meat. I nudged the bits around the bowl before moving to the gooey orange mass on the plate beside my soup bowl. I wondered, if the goo were green would Auntie still try to call it carrots.

Somewhere in the middle of the goo stirring, Mother remarked how fatigued I appeared and mentioned retiring early.

"Maybe you should sleep in your dress tonight," Auntie piped in then. "It is the third outfit of the day is it not?" Her words scratched across my mind.

Auntie leaned far over on her cane. She reached beneath the folds of the linen table covering and pulled out a crumpled, muddied, still somewhat soggy wad that had been my morning attire. Auntie's eyes flashed lightning.

"Decided to take a little wade in the river at recess did you? Didn't think old Auntie's eyes were so sharp as to find your not-so-well-concealed evidence?" She was fully out of her seat, shaking the wad of clothing in one hand.

Her cane rattled the floorboards.

Muddy droplets spattered as she shambled forward, spotting the white tablecloth, the sleek floor, even the old hag herself. As if the clothes held some VooDoo power over my body, I too began to shake.

"Emily." Mother's astonishment broke the spell. "How on earth did you manage to get your clothing so filthy in only a twenty-minute recess? I didn't even think your little legs could carry you to the river and back in that amount of time."

This further agitated Auntie. "Twenty minutes? Twenty minutes! You were graciously given twenty minutes to refresh from your studies and this is how you occupied yourself? By soiling one of your best dresses!"

I wanted to tell her that nearly all my dresses could be considered bests, but I was too weary and too terrified to dare make witty comments. Trolls are not fond of wit. Then Auntie did something remarkable. She granted my only wish for the evening.

"I think retiring early is quite a good idea for such a filthy, naughty, little piggy." The old woman shook her cane, nearly toppling herself in the process.

Not about to stick around, I miraculously found strength of body to pump my weary legs up to my warm safe bed as fast as they would willingly carry me.

I was pulling on my nightgown when I heard Mother's familiar rap on the door.

"May I come in?" She was already part way in the room.

From within my nightshirt, I mumbled a greeting.

Mother helped me push my head through the opening of the nightshirt.

"I think it is about time to buy some new

clothes." Mother turned me around to eye the fit.

I pulled away gently. "Now is probably not the best time to discuss a new wardrobe with Auntie," I reminded her.

"Oh, now, Emily, I wouldn't worry too much about that." A sly smirk danced onto her face. "By tomorrow Auntie won't remember what you wore, nor whether you got it dirty or not." she pushed a curl from my eyes. "I'll have the clothes and her memory of the whole episode washed away by sunrise."

We both fell into relieved giggles. The laugh at Auntie's expense continued due to tickling. By the time we heard the familiar shuffle thump coming down the hallway, we had worked into an all out pillow brawl.

Mother hurried to tuck me under the covers and kiss me off to sleep. I heard her in the darkness, slipping out the door just in time to meet Auntie there. I listened as Mother turned the key in the lock.

"Good idea, Lucy dear, locking that filthy child away." Auntie's cane rapped at the foot of the doorframe. "Should be done as often as I did to you. Look how you turned out." the old woman cackled.

"Yes, Auntie. I quite agree, Auntie." It was Mother's usual mantra. "Cleanliness is next to Godliness." She added for good measure.

Mother and I knew the real reason she locked the door. I heard the key ping to the threshold. A moment later, Mother claimed clumsiness and feigned the key's retrieval. I leaned over the edge of the bed and peered across the room. The bit of metal glinted through the gap beneath the door. A fluffy white feather shook loose from my curls and floated past my nose. It landed among its friends upon the floor. I stifled a giggle.

Why did they not make the casings of feather pillows out of sterner stuff?

In the silent comfort of my dark room, I mulled over the day's events. I considered all logical explanations. That I had fallen into the river and hit the rocks was at the top of the list. I read somewhere that a hit on the head could cause hallucinations. I felt the back of my head and all around beneath my cloud of curls. No tender swollen hills. I assumed it would have to be a really amazing smack to see what I had seen.

I pushed the bedside curtain aside. In the moonglow, I analyzed the bruises on my palms. They could've been caused in attempting to catch myself from falling. I clenched my fingers lightly into my palms. My nails were rough, a couple even broken to the quick. That could have been caused by hitting the river rocks. Auntie and Mother had taught me very well. Logical explanation was slowly winning against instinct. Instinct was having a temper tantrum.

On the way to church some Sundays, I would imagine playing with the other children I saw from my view out the car's rear windows. From between the lace eyelets and frills of my Sunday bonnet, I would wonder at their world. My curiosity danced with visions of skipping ropes and hula-hoops, balls and bats and games of jacks. How different their world was from mine. How alive. The children of the village lived in a world of popguns, endless chaos and enjoyment. My world was all books and old records that played scratchy minuets from times more bygone than the manor. I had some dolls, leftovers from Mother's childhood, and dress-up clothes, mostly worn attire from Mother's equally bygone youth. More often than not, my world was silent and solitary—except in my mind.

Everyday, I hoped for friends my own age. Everyday, I hoped to live the fairytales that overtook my bookshelves. By some strange occurrence I had been granted both, but I refused to acknowledge that it had all been real.

I must have dozed off sometime in the middle of the conflict between my mind and my heart. My dreams were molded by the events of the day and the battle that raged over them.

I was in the grotto beneath the bridge, again. This time it was not so dark. The shelves glittered with a greenish aura from some unseen source. The mossy carpet sparkled with dew that scattered like diamonds and bounced about to sing against the walls when I kicked the beads with the tips of my toes.

The collection in the walls drew my gaze. Dolls, tops, toy cars, shoes, skates, balls, bats and hula-hoops cluttered the crevices. My eyes danced over everything a child could ask for, then fell on something peeking from behind the sail of a tiny boat. Dewdrop diamonds scurried from my feet as I moved to investigate.

I moved the sailboat gently. It was someone's priceless heirloom. I felt it. I set it gingerly onto a nearby shelf and returned my focus to the object it had guarded.

The rattle resembled a palm-sized jingle-bell.

The metal was coated with chipped white paint. The end of the handle had a hole with a tattered shred of faded pink ribbon hanging in a sad bow. I cradled the tiny object as if some lost key to an ancient civilization.

"That belonged to Tierannie, the lost troll."

I turned to see who had spoken and fell out of bed.

CHAPTER THREE:
THE PICNIC, THE GARDENER, AND THE ADVENTURE BEGINS

What a vivid dream.

I rubbed my elbow where it had struck the floor. The sun burned the room a pale shade of yellow. I crawled my way back into bed, across the freezing, feather-scattered floor, and noticed something jutting from beneath my pillow. I tugged at the strip of cloth and the pink bow came undone as I pulled free the rattle from my dream. Instinct did a joyful dance on the back of my brain as logic was completely overruled.

Mother knocked and whispered at the door.

For no reason that I could think of, I stuffed the rattle back into its comfortable hiding place and scooted on my knees to the door. Instead of unlocking the door, I knocked the key under the door to Mother.

The key turned in the lock and a moment later Mother's worried eyes stared down at me. She sidled past my crouched form and slid the door closed. Her long skirt fluffed the feathers away in a circle around where she sat down on the floor.

"Emily, are you okay?" She cupped my chin and turned my face to hers. "Did you have a bad dream?"

My world was becoming more the stuff of fairy tales, just as I had always wished it to. Nonsense was winning over commonsense. All I could do was lift my elbow to Mother's attention. "I fell off the bed."

She kissed the bruised joint and handed me a fresh white pillow casing. She had made two new ones from an old sheet after Auntie had gone to sleep. The two of us moved about the room, gathering feathers from the oddest places. Slowly, the dream, just like any other, faded. I giggled and danced with Mother, harvesting our garden of down. Soon, we had two stuffed and fluffed pillows ready to be sewn shut. From her apron pocket, Mother pulled a spool of deep blue thread stuck with a pair of needles.

"Usually I would just as easily have stitched these shut with the machine, but it is a lazy Saturday and something told me we needed the time to talk. Besides, Auntie will be quite pleased if we tell her you have been practicing your mending."

In the end, it was always about keeping Auntie happy.

I hated sewing, but I loved spending time alone with Mother. She was so beautiful and so cheerful when Auntie was absent. I smiled as I watched her enjoy every stitch. I wondered how someone so wonderful could be kept trapped by someone as cruel as Auntie. It wasn't really a logical world at all, when I thought about such things. It was just sad.

"Mother?" I broke the beautiful silence.

Her green eyes looked up at me and burned with joy.

"Why do you stay with Auntie?"

The joyful blaze flickered with a solemn glow. She smiled. "I owe Auntie everything. You know that." I knew the statement was more for her benefit than mine, but I nodded.

"After my mother passed away . . . " She edged closer to me on the floor and petted my curls. ". . . my father lost himself in his grief. He had lost the most beloved thing in the world to him and it was because of me." Her tears welled but she did not stop her story. "Auntie cursed her sister's vanity and blamed it for my mother being so frail. A creature who flitted all her energy on being pretty could never have the strength to carry a child through the term, according to her. Out of the goodness of her heart, Auntie took me in and raised me."

"More likely she was forever jealous of her sister and thought hiding the evidence of her beauty away from the world was the best sort of revenge." I interrupted.

I had never told Mother such things before. I had no idea why I told her now.

The light went out behind the glowing green buds of Mother's eyes. "Don't say such things, Emily." There was a coldness in her voice I had not heard before. "Don't ever say such things."

I had struck a resounding chord though and could not let go. "Certainly, when you were a child she took you in, when no other would. Just as you did for me. Certainly, she cared for you and gave you all she felt you needed to remain healthy, but did she ever really let you grow? Have you ever been truly happy?" I punched a dent into the pillow in my lap. "Haven't you ever wanted to run away, to be free, to be loved?"

Mother's fingers tensed on the casing in her lap.

"I don't know how you do it, Mother. I don't know how you live beneath her cane day in and day out. I don't know." I stood, letting the pillow thump to the floor. "And I don't know about you, but someday, I am going to get out."

Silent tears leaked down both our cheeks. The light had returned to her eyes.

Her fingertips touched my lips. "When you are able to leave, I will leave."

She waited for me to be seated again. "There was a time, shortly before you arrived, when I planned to go far from this house and its silent sorrows." She wiped aside my tears and petted my curls. "Even though I am not free, with you here I am loved and free to love."

In a sudden movement, Mother stood, her sewing tumbling from her lap. "Oh my! The gardener!" As if freed from a spell, she gathered up our sewing and set the finished pillows haphazardly on the bed.

"He'll be here any moment and I . . . look at me," She gestured to her kerchief-tied hair and stained apron. "I am a fright!"

She left me standing alone in the center of my pale room uncertain whether to smile or weep. I fell down laughing.

Of course! The gardener.

When my laughter subsided, I prepared for the day. My imagination was still throwing a victory party over logic and reality. They wanted a prize. From my wardrobe, I pulled a deep blue dress with too many frills and bows. Did all little girls only own dresses? Without destroying the dress, I popped as many bows off as possible and hid them in my winter coat pockets. Even though my legs would be too warm, I pulled on a pair of winter knee socks in navy blue. A dark blue beret to cover my hair and black shoes completed the outfit. I needed to hide any dirt.

Into my apron went a full roll of parcel ribbon and a book of matches that had been ferreted away. The strange old rattle—key to all this absurdity—I pulled from its nest of blankets and tucked into a pocket.

Finished with the important business, I climbed onto the mound of pillows at the head of my bed and nudged aside the folds of the window curtain. After a moment of daydreaming, I heard the familiar rattle-clunk of Sir Trevor's steed making its way up the drive.

The late morning sunlight glinted off the beast's dark flanks. Sir Trevor's hands rested loosely on the reins.

As this rusty but gallant steed approached, the squeak of the palace gate below the watchtower drew my attention I spied the scarlet tresses of the Jungle's princess. Though her face was hidden, I could tell she was glowing. Auntie would not approve.

The steed shuddered and came to rest at the gates.

Mother stepped off the porch and waved. "Hello." I heard from my perch.

Trevor, who had emerged from his metal steed, nearly impaled them both as he leaned against his pile of rakes, clippers, saws, and shovels. He ducked and swept Mother out of harm's way, just as the arsenal clattered to the ground. Mother and he blushed and brushed at one another.

I giggled furiously.

This same scene played out nearly every Saturday. Trevor would watch Mother go about her weekend chores and would carelessly clip too much off a topiary here, or bump his rattling lawn cutter into a tree stump there.

Mother was not much better. While she had far more grace than her sweet-yet-clumsy, would-be suitor, she made use of it all just to hang the laundry on the line properly, or to keep from dropping dishes as she watched through the kitchen window.

Auntie found it positively disgusting, and said so often. I found the whole ordeal quite amusing. I saw how the two giggled and blushed and found ways of brushing knuckles—beautiful, graceful Mother, Princess of the Jungle and silly, offbeat Sir Trevor the Clumsy.

I sighed, shook my head, and turned away from the window to make my way to the kitchen. Mother laid out a picnic every Saturday to share with the gardener, but little of it was edible. A gourmet cook every other day of the week, on Saturdays she may as well have made mud pies. There were always strange problems with Mother's cooking whenever Trevor was on her mind. Egg salad was prone to crunchy bits, lemonade was more lemon than ade, and one never quite knew what to make of the cookies or muffins that found their way into the mix. To say the pair distracted one another was to say the ants in the garden were distracted by Saturday picnics.

Auntie stood in the doorway. I could only see half her face from the angle she was leaning, but her scowl still made me back away. Still spying on Mother and Trevor, I scuttled on hands and knees as quietly as possible to the pantry door. I hated being locked in the pantry in the dark, but any monster that may have been nesting there was most certainly less frightening than Auntie pre-coffee and post-Trevor-spotting.

I batted at the darkness for the light string. It found me instead as I swiped past it once and my hand was coiled in its grasp as it came back around. The light snapped on. I blinked.

The treasures revealed by the illumination were far more delectable than those of Tut's tomb when the first explorers feasted their eyes on them. I pulled a fresh jar of apricot preserves and a thick loaf of bread from off the shelf. Who needs utensils? I popped the seal on the preserves and swirled a chunk of crusty soft bread in the sweet jelly. Paradise is a well-stocked pantry.

After breakfast I made sure to stow the evidence in the back of the pantry where Auntie's cane could not pass then, I slipped out of the kitchen like a robber on the run.

Auntie sat, molded into a scowling gargoyle, perched in her wicker rocker on the stone slab at the entrance to the Jungle. Mother busied herself with watering the roses closest to Trevor, trying not to be utterly conspicuous, while Trevor mended a pillar on the temple. It had taken both Mother and Trevor to save the temple and convince Auntie that a gazebo belonged in any proper yard. More than once I had overheard Mother reminisce the elegant weddings held beneath the octagonal roof in days past.

As much as I wanted to return to my adventure back to the bridge, it looked as if the adult obstacles would not be removed until after the picnic.

I busied myself as far from Auntie as possible, but close enough to read everyone's expressions. There was no better entertainment on a Saturday morning than the drama these adults so willingly played out for me. I sat just out of Mother's line of sight and pretended to be absorbed by a troop of ants conquering a tuft of grass. I whiled away intermissions making dandelion crowns. If I had come prepared, I could have staked out over the binding of a book closer to Auntie without much fuss. Today, I had left my books upstairs; none of the adventures came close to the one in my mind about the grotto and all the possibilities it held.

"Hey, Emily! Sprite!" I shook away the phantom shelves of toys and gazed at Trevor's outstretched hand. "Is there any food in dreamland, or are you going to join us for lunch?"

I grinned at the shadow of his sun-haloed face, took his hand and let him swing me to my feet.

Mother brought out a small card table and set it in front of Auntie's scowling figure. Mother laid out her disaster-ridden spread, then brought out a kitchen stool, fluffed her skirts, and sit beside

Auntie. I settled cross-legged on a footstool and casually slid Auntie's cane from the arm of the rocker and under the table. Trevor slumped into an old porch chair as far from Auntie as possible.

He grinned when he saw me remove the cane. Auntie always seemed to hit him when she was aiming for me.

Today's menu consisted of Mother's unusual egg salad. There were, to her credit, far fewer crunchy bits usual. She had decided to add green olives, though they had the chewy consistency of green apple jellybeans I had been hoarding since last Easter. No one seemed to notice and I certainly didn't mind.

Lunch went smoothly even with Auntie guarding against flirtatious behavior between Mother and Trevor. Auntie's eyes were not that great and Trevor was a practiced charmer. Most days this would be amusing, but today I was focused on the bridge. I gulped my lemonade in one sour-faced slurp that made my nose burn and my eyes water. I tucked three cookies into my pocket and slipped off the porch.

"Emily!" Mother tore her gaze from Trevor. "Where are you off to?"

"Just to play, Mother!" I spun full circle to wave and continued on, holding my beret to my head.

I refused to give Auntie a chance to get out of her chair to stop me. This mission was far too important. By the time I tumbled to a halt at the foot of the bridge, I was panting and my stockings had shimmied down to my ankles.

The hole in the bridge had grown into a chasm. Only the two ornate parallel arcs and a bit of stone at each side of the river bound the bridge together. This was not going to be as easy as last time, and that had not been easy at all.

I tested one granite-orbed pillar, then the other. There was still a chance of success. I had spent all morning working out the variables and possible routes to a very illogical entrance into an impossible location, but I was certain I had figured it out. If not, things would end in a messy and possibly painful manner.

I pulled my beret tight around my ears and stepped up to the railing. I hopped, and swung, and straddled as before, this time scooting across to the highest point on the arch. I tipped my head forward and let the hat tumble into my waiting hands. From my apron pocket, I pulled the parcel string, hoping there would be enough.

Using the best knots mother taught, I tied one end of the string to the bridge, tucking it through the apron strings and unrolling as much as I thought necessary. With the matchbook rolled tight into the beret and stuffed into my pocket, I was ready.

Not really, but if I stopped now I would be frozen on the bridge forever. Balancing on the rail, overlooking the center of the narrow river, I opened my arms wide and . . .

"Emily!" Mother's voice ripped across the open field.

Turning fast, I glimpsed her barreling toward the bridge, her skirts flying, Trevor close behind. My shoes slid out from under my legs. The world tipped. Ripples of the stream sped toward me. Inches above the water I closed my eyes and prepared for impact.

The river burst around me, sucking me down. My eyes and lungs ached to open as bubbles glugged against my flailing limbs.

Time felt strange in the moment before enough air entered my lungs to allow the wind to be knocked out of me as I struck the mossy carpet. I grunted into the moist floor. My arms twisted and pushed until I flopped over. I dug the empty spool from under my throbbing hip and searched the ceiling for some sign of the string. Panic pushed away the aches as I shot upright to watch the swaying twine far above my reach.

"Back again?" The boy who called himself a troll crossed his arms. "After all that work last time, I would have thought we had seen the last of you."

CHAPTER FOUR:
BURN, PILLAGE, AND PLUNDER

He stood with his arms crossed, a cocky half-grin curling his narrow lips. His hair dirty, and the same clothes as before making it seem like he really did live in a tunnel. I wondered where the other two were. I preferred their company.

He dropped his arms to his sides and stared at my hand, or rather what it held.

"Put that back!" He advanced.

I sidestepped and cradled the rattle to my chest.

"A little late." I spat. "I had it all night. It fell out of my dream."

Confusion twisted his face.

Payback, I thought, for our first meeting.

He continued advancing. I circled away, creating a strange dance. Two children vying for a baby toy.

"What is so wrong about my having this rattle? The way I see it, if it was in my dream, it belongs to me." Maybe that would unbalance him enough for me to figure out a plan. I had not thought what I would do if I made it this far. "Where and what is this place, anyway?"

I shook the rattle at him but snapped it away when he swiped for it.

"This is the Grotto of the Findings." He eyed the rattle. "It's where we keep all the lost toys that fall into the rivers."

I dodged another swipe. "Fine. And who are you?"

"You're the intruder." He lunged. "Tell me first."

"Fine then. My name is Emily." I ducked.

He tumbled over me and into a wall.

"Burn." He rubbed his nose and righted himself. "My name is Burn."

"Well, that's a weird name." I forgot a moment about the rattle.

Burn would have had it too if the twins had not tumbled in.

"And we . . . "

"Are . . . "

"Pillage and Plunder." They introduced one another and with synchronized bows rolled into somersaults and landed at my feet.

"Are you . . .?" Pillage, the female twin, grabbed the hem of my apron.

"Really . . .." Plunder tugged at the opposite side.

"The lost . . ." Pillage reached for my hair.

"Troll, Tierannie?" Plunder finished the question with a tilt of his head.

I was dizzy already, but they continued their verbal volley

"What . . . " Plunder's eyes turned skyward.

"Is it like . . ." Pillage raised my arm with hers.

"Up There?" In unison, the two gazed at the

ceiling of the grotto.

I was not sure I could keep up with this verbal volley. "I am not sure if I am this lost troll,"

"Tierannie," Burn interjected, as if to join the game.

At least the twins served as distraction and barrier against Burn's advance. "Tierannie, yes. Right." I corrected. "Anyway, I don't know if I am." I caught Burn glaring again. "But I would like to find out. I would also like to know anything you can tell me about where we are now."

If Burn was not going to tell me anything, I would move to more willing springs of information. "And in return, I will tell you anything you care to know about Up There." I pointed to the shining hole above.

"Oh!" They bounded in circles and took hold of my arms. "We will show you everything!"

They ushered past Burn, who turned an appropriate color for his name and moved toward a tattered curtain on a far wall.

I stopped.

"I thought the only way out was through that tiny opening in the ceiling?" I glared at Burn.

"It is," he said, his tone cool, "if you want to go back to the surface world." He stalked up to the curtain and tore it from its rings. "This is the way to the Queen's Hall."

The light beyond blinded me. Even after my eyes adjusted, I blinked. Whatever small portion of Logical Explanation was pulling for a comeback was knocked out by Vivid Imagination.

Though my eyes barely adjusted to the brightness of this new and different world, still they could not help but frolic in wonder. Only in the Jungle had I seen such green life or smelled such sweet and earthy perfumes. There was a clear difference between this Jungle and mine—no glass. As far as I could see—which granted was not very far considering the thick and tangled braids of green my eyes worked to peer through—there were no walls here.

Burn came up alongside me and pushed my jaw from the floor. "The flies here are not very friendly. Probably best not to catch them."

I stuck my tongue out at him, but heeded the warning. I had learned from my storybooks, the more beautiful a place, the more deadly. I was grateful for the warning, but I did not have to admit it out loud.

Burn turned to me once more before stepping into the Jungle. "There are much worse things that lie ahead in the Jungle."

"Is where we are going dangerous?" I knew before I voiced it, it was probably a foolish question, but I had a feeling it would be my first of many, so why not get started.

"The Grotto, where you fell in, is a protected place. It is a sacred hiding for the most precious of Troll treasures." Burn grinned. "Unlike in the Jungle, where danger lurks at every turn. I come here often, but for Pillage and Plunder traveling here it is a training session."

The younger children nodded vigorously.

"The bridge above this grotto was supposed to belong to a Troll, but she disappeared before the Queen could bring her through the opening. Now it is just a great story, and a great adventure to quest here." Burn stood a little taller as he explained. "I have been here hundreds of times."

This Jungle journey was just one more way for Burn to give me the creeps, and one more thing I would have to prove I was just as equally capable of, I thought.

"Don't . . . " Pillage gripped my sleeve.

"Worry . . . " Plunder attached himself to the other.

"We don't . . . " The pair leaned in close.

"Like . . . " They lowered their voices.

"The Jungle . . . " And shuddered.

"Either." They released their grip, though only slightly.

"It's not that bad." Burn scowled, "As long as you stick to the path. Grow up you two!"

The twins cowered behind me and stuck out their tongues. "We can't."

Burn took a sudden step toward them and they ducked fully behind me. I could not help but return the snide grin he had given me in the Grotto. It seemed his little minions were on my side now.

He narrowed his eyes and walked on. "Come on. I haven't got all day to play stupid games with stupid children and a stupid girl." Under his breath, though loud enough to hear, he added, "We will see you hide behind when you really need help."

The path was barely wide enough for the twins and I to walk abreast—which they insisted upon doing. The trail of fine colored sand was no trouble at all to follow. Entranced, I watched footprints in front of me change color as Burn walked ahead. It was wondrous! The path was a mottled rainbow of lines and swirls, surrounding the solid colored footprints. Blue. Green. Yellow. Orange. Red. The colors cycled like the arcs of a reverse rainbow. I turned my head to see if the twins and I made the same impression.

How odd.

Instead of a trail of overlapping, path-wide footprints behind us, there was nothing at all. The sand behind was clear of any markings having slithered to its original blur. I faced the direction the twins guided and observed the fleeting marks following Burn. I noticed something even more bizarre. This set was not alone. On either side, the prints were flanked by smaller sets. Moreover, the middle footprints were shaped as if a shoed foot made them. Burn was not wearing any shoes. I looked down at my own feet nested comfortably in buckled shoes. The twins were barefoot and, as I watched, another row of prints appear, the smaller prints were indeed from bare feet. I halted mid-step. The twins swung on my arms and bounced off one another and onto their bottoms, thumping soundly onto the path.

"Ow!" They rubbed their heads and rears in unison.

Burn spun on his heels and threw his arms up in exasperation. "Now, what is the problem?"

That is when I saw it. A trail of rainbow-hued footprints leading out into the Jungle ahead. The prints did not appear in our wake, they were there before us. Burn sauntered to where I stood staring into the distance, about-faced and followed my gaze.

"Oh," his same haughty grin returned, "I suppose to an outsider that might seem a bit odd." He patted my shoulder condescendingly. "Poor girl. I bet you haven't a clue what to make of The Follow the Path." He extended his arm. "It is very simple. This path already knows where we are going and it knows the way. Though, I am sure it is confusing to a poor stupid girl." He poked a finger at my forehead.

I batted his hand away and continued down the path. We resumed our previous formation, once Burn stopped snickering.

Pillage whispered in my ear after a time, "I think he likes you." Her bright little eyes glittered.

"What? Who?" I hissed, harsher than intended.

"Burn, silly." Her little nose wrinkled up. "I think he has a crush on you."

Was she daft? She must have missed the treatment I was getting from the boy.

"He hasn't stopped talking about you since you climbed back to Up There." Conspiracy colored her tone and her eyes darted left and right. "Boys are very silly, but because of Plunder, I know what they think."

"Hush!" Burn stopped short.

Pillage covered her mouth, thinking she had been found out, but it was not Pillage Burn heard. He pointed to his ears. We all listened. Singing? Where was it coming from?

The beautiful sound lulled my senses. I closed my eyes to the clear, floating sounds. I could not understand the words gliding into the air around us. I didn't need to. I could feel the notes. Twisted ribbons tangled my mind. Tendrils of blue-green high notes wrapped in and around bobbing burgundy altos. Angelic blue arias in high C soared overhead and dipped into a web of spiraling fingertips caressing my cheeks, eyes and hair. I could feel the song pull me off the ground. My feet and legs cupped in the firm tenor hold, a rippling watercolor carpet in heavy greens, blues and reds. The sounds tugged at my clothes and skin, enclosing me in a painfully beautiful prison of sound and song. Somewhere in the undertones pricked the voices of Burn, Pillage and Plunder. They sang my name. So did the voice, much more lovely and clear.

Whiney, whimpering yellows of the twin's trailed away first. Black-brown spears from Burn's boyish screams were swallowed suddenly by flaring blue and yellow arias. The voice, singing my name, bloomed a pale lotus before my eyes. I reached toward the vision and the sound. The image exploded and suddenly I could not hear anything. Deafness rang in my ears following the overwhelming sound. My eyes shot open.

I shrieked.

I clapped both hands over my mouth to keep from losing Mother's egg salad. I stared into the bulging dead eyes of a horrendous grey-green serpent. The severed head lay in my lap.

A naked foot kicked it away.

I followed the foot to the face of its owner. Burn stood over me, bloodied blade in hand. His ears were blocked with what looked to be the feet from a small stuffed animal.

Pillage and Plunder ducked into view behind Burn's elbows. They too had ears full of fluff. The twins fell from Burn's side and tumbled into my lap. I could see their small shoulders bobbing as if they were crying, but I could not hear the sobs. I felt my ears and found them walled with stuffing. Burn plucked a pair of dismembered stuffed rabbit ears from the sides of my head and dropped them into my lap.

"I told you to stick to the path." Burn wiped his blade against the monster's hide, then stalked off.

The twins pulled me back onto the path and hurried me along.

"I told you he liked having you around." Pillage smiled, though unshed tears still shivered in her wide eyes.

Not letting me be eaten by a nasty singing monster did not exactly scream "Be My Valentine," but it did suggest Burn had a good side. I sprinted to catch up to him.

"Hey." I panted, putting a hand on his shoulder. I took my hand away when I saw his eyes. Whether from tears or anger, they were incredibly red.

"What do you want now?" He practically spit the words.

"Look." What I wanted to say was it was all his idea to bring me along in the first place instead of letting me just go home. But I pushed down my rising anger. "I just want to thank you."

Pillage and Plunder eyed the exchange carefully as they caught up.

"Yeah. Well." He rubbed the back of his head. "It wasn't really your fault. I should have told you about the sirens."

I gauged his features. He seemed sincere. "I don't know what I did to start us off as enemies, but, it was really brave of you to take down that monster." I held out a hand. "Friends?"

He stared a long moment at my hand. Pillage

and Plunder seemed to have stopped breathing as they awaited Burn's reaction.

"Friends." He spit into his palm and gripped my hand. "But, do not listen to anything she tells you. Girls are more disgusting than sirens. "He jabbed a finger at Pillage

Pillage stuck her tongue out.

We were all moving on the right track again, but it was hard to tell how far we traveled. The tangle of vines and trees looked the same along either side of the path.

The encounter with the siren made me worry what other deadly creatures hid in the tangled green that flanked the path.

I quickened my pace to walk beside Burn. "Not that I am in a hurry, or scared, or anything, but how much time does it take to get through this jungle?"

"Doesn't really matter, time doesn't move the same Up There."

His words sunk in. "What do you mean time moves different down here?"

"I said it moves different Up There. Down here it moves just fine." He pointed to a glow in the leaves ahead. "As for how much longer we will be in the Jungle, there's your answer. 'Are we there yet,' usually pushes things. This is actually the longest it's ever taken. Generally, Pillage and Plunder start asking 'are we there yet' moments after starting out. I think they wanted to take you on the scenic route."

I cut in front of Burn and glared at him. "Why didn't you just say something in the beginning?"

He shrugged.

I could feel the heat rising to my cheeks. "If all it

takes is asking, 'are we there yet', why did we walk so long?"

"Because I like the Jungle." His cocky grin returned. "I have traveled the path every day since I was younger than the twins. I know all its tricks."

"All the tricks? Like that siren!" I was fuming.

"That was a close one. Sirens can be fun." Burn nodded.

"Fun."

I probably would have broken our friendship truce about then if the twins had not come bounding up singing. "We're here! We're here!" The pair blurred past in their rush to reach the clearing.

Burn stepped around me and rested his hands atop his shaggy hair.

My stomach fluttered and the anger at Burn dissipated. I brushed past him and took off after the twins. I was about to meet the Queen of the Trolls.

CHAPTER FIVE:
THE MOON, THE STARS, AND THE QUEEN

I burst through the opening in the leaves and plunged headlong into water.

The glow I had seen from the clearing was the reflection of light off the surface of a vast underground lake. Fortunately, the water was only waist deep. It felt so clean and pure. For a moment I forgot I had fallen into a murky river, traversed a dangerous jungle and nearly been eaten by a giant singing snake.

I also forgot about Burn and the twins. A splash from behind washed over my head and shoulders, bringing it all back. Burn, with hands behind his head, grinned from ear to ear. He showed off the gaps from lost baby teeth with his crooked smile. He launched himself into the air. I was pulled and pushed clear by two identical, clean and glowing children. Burn, hitting the water with a tsunami sized splash, fully submerged under the glittering surface. When he burst forth, glowing with cleanliness, only his gap-toothed grin was recognizable.

Pillage's corn-colored hair, pulled up in pale green lace bows, cascaded down in a pair of ringlet-curled pigtails. Her pink face and shining blue eyes peered at me from under thick cut bangs. Plunder's cherubic face smiled under a neat bowl cut. Both were clothed in the same minty hue, Pillage in a coverall dress and white pouf-sleeved blouse, Plunder in shorts and white button down shirt. They looked ready to go to Easter Mass.

So did Burn.

He did not seem as thrilled as they about being clean and properly dressed. He pushed his bowl cut bangs to one side, and tugged at the long sleeved, dark green version of Plunder's attire.

When Burn noticed my expression of awe, he knocked my mouth closed again. "There are no flies here." He looked around. "You may as well keep the trap shut."

"I can't help it." They all looked so completely different.

"Her Majesty," offered Pillage.

"Likes it . . ." Plunder combed at his hair.

"When we . . ." Pillage bounced her ringlets.

"Dress our best . . ." Plunder straightened his collar.

"In her presence." Pillage curtsied.

I hoped that my outfit would be good enough since I had not brought a change of clothing along with me. Inspection of my reflection in the calming water disclosed I too was no longer soiled, nor missing bows and lace. The color of my dress had shifted from its original deep navy-blue to the same green as Burn's pants.

Shock and confusion warred over me. "Why green?"

"Because," answered a new and beautiful voice, "green is my favorite color."

I turned toward the voice, half expecting another siren. I was more than grateful to be mistaken.

Red gold hair swept the surface of the lake like a glittering fog trailing behind and over the train of her emerald gown. Eyes that matched the vibrant green of her gown, smiled at me. She approached with the grace of a swan. From beneath the water she retrieved a round white river rock. Studying the stone a moment, she sailed it into the air above. My eyes caught the stone in flight and followed it. Far below the arcing ceiling, yet high above the lake, the stone froze. It dazzled my eyes as I watched it turn slowly as if on an invisible thread. All around, the spreading ceiling grew dark, to reveal bits of crystal glittering above us. Suspended by some invisible web, the night sky blossomed, created before my very eyes.

Burn lifted my jaw shut again. Only, this time he did not say anything. He too gazed in awe.

The Queen floated toward us, her beautiful smile washed our minds clean of the terrible Jungle, leaving only the vague scars of experience.

She extended a slender pale hand. I had learned from fairy tales never to trust anything beautiful, and less so a queen, but this was more real than any fairy tale.

When I took her hand the weight of the outside world lifted. Water lapped at the soles of my shimmering shoes as I stood on its surface. With my free hand, I felt the fabric of my apron. I was dry. I could not tear my gaze from the beautiful Queen. At the edge of my view the others walked on the surface of the lake. Behind the Queen and on all sides, a crowd gathered. Faces, all my age and younger, even those of the infants crawling at our feet, were magnificently beautiful and smiling.

"Welcome home, Tierannie." The room erupted in a chorus of applause and cheers.

It was then I remembered the rattle. I reached down into the folds of my apron pocket. It was gone. The object that brought me this far, I had lost somewhere in the dreadful Jungle.

I dropped to my knees and pressed my hands against the smooth surface of the lake searching. The cheers ebbed only a little while I sought for my prize, and the Queen did not move. I did not want to look at her though for fear I had lost this important object.

"Here." Burn poked at my arm. "I suppose, this is yours, after all."

Relief flowed over me when I stood and saw the rattle in his grasp. I took the rattle from his hands and held it high. It seemed the proper thing to do. I offered a smile and a thankful nod to Burn. Another wave of cheers and applause shook the moon and stars. Pillage and Plunder joined hands and happily danced around me. Even Burn wore a look of pride. I was one of them, approved by her majesty herself. The dancing and cheering continued many minutes. As smoothly as she had arrived and pulled me from the water the Queen turned and her great train of red and green followed her to the opalescent throne at the far end of the room. Her departure caused the lake to ripple and lose solidity. As she sat the spell was broken.

With a splash, all were soaked again.

The twins waded over and took my hands. A throng of children crowded toward an arch at the far end of the cavern. I turned back to see the Queen. She smiled and curled her hand into a small wave. She seemed so young, yet so familiar.

She looked just like Mother!

I tried to pry free from the twins. To go back. The flowing crowd of chatter and laughter moved me into the opening and beyond.

I hoped that what waited on the other side of the darkness was nowhere near as bad as the Jungle. I felt safe in assuming it was not as wonderful as the throne room, but if Burn and the twins were eager to go, then I would follow. As we waded out of the lake, the savory aroma of cooking chicken reminded me that I had not eaten since the picnic. Even if time moved differently, it still moved. My stomach growled.

"Dinner!" the twins called out.

CHAPTER SIX:
DINNER PARTIES AND RESCUE PARTIES

I blinked out of the darkness to find myself in an even larger cavern. Stalactites dripped from the vaulted ceilings and from each spire a single candle swung in a small wooden holder. My eyes followed the mad pulley system web that strung each one together. The mathematics to create such webbing dizzied my brain.

As I twisted to take in the maze I lost my balance.

"Whoa there." Strong hands steadied me.

I brought my gaze back to earth and found myself leaning into the arms of a very tall, very gangly, hook-nosed man.

"Can't have the guest of honor cracking her curly head on the dining hall floor now can we."

While the rest of his features made me question whether or not I should run, his eyes made me feel perfectly safe. His vibrant blue eyes glittered beneath a shaggy mane of brown. He smiled exactly as I imagined a loving older brother would.

He helped me regain balance, then stood. I thought him tall when hunched over. At his full height I feared he might bump the stalactite candelabras. Other children crowded, inquiring what there was to eat and how soon it would be served. The giant's smile expanded even further, showing snaggled, yet gleaming white teeth. I could not keep the smile from my face, as well.

"Well, if all of you mischievous little Trollings will scurry off to your seats, then you shall see what's for eating tonight." And with one playful shooing motion into the crowd, he chased all the children to the waiting picnic style tables and benches.

The twins pulled me into a seat across from Burn. A group of boys, about Burn's age, pushed into the benches, poking and being rude to one another. Plunder stood on the bench and tried to join in the game. The older boys ignored him until one decided to give Plunder's wrist a wicked twist in his hands. A harsh red ring bloomed on his pale skin. Plunder crashed back into his spot beside me and held the wound under my nose. I prepared to hug away tears.

"Look, Tierannie! Look what they did to me!" His face glowed. "Isn't it great? I am one of them now! For real this time!"

I turned to Pillage. She rotated a finger in the air beside her ear. "Burn's Boys are strange."

I looked at Burn for explanation. He flashed his Puckish grin and crossed his skinny arms. The boys followed suit. Burn and his 'tribe' were typical boys. Rowdy, loud, and dirty even after a bath in the Queen's lake.

When the boys were finally seated, I asked Burn,

"Who is the very tall man all the children are so fond of?"

Burn grinned, clearly happy to offer information on something else I was clueless about. "That is Drake. He is the caretaker of the space between the bridges and . . ." he sniffed the air. ". . . the best cook in the entire world."

"Really? The best?" My stomach growled though, betraying my doubt.

Burn leaned across the table. "He is also a giant. One of the last."

"He also . . ." Pillage leaned into my ear.

"Has a . . ." Plunder leaned in as well.

"Crush on . . ." Pillage squeaked out the words.

"The Queen." Plunder scrunched up his face.

They shared the sentence but not the sentiment. Pillage continued to gaze star-eyed and blushing. Plunder made terrible mock kissing faces.

"You think everyone has a crush on everyone." Burn scoffed at Plunder.

The boy's patted his back and stuck their tongues out at Pillage.

She gave it right back to them.

"He does hang around the Queen quite a bit though." One of the boys nodded.

"And he gets all weird when she is around." Another made a doe-eyed face.

Burn shoved them both. The poking and nudging began anew with a roar of laughter.

Like brothers, I thought, though I knew it could not be since they all looked so very different. Some had curly hair, some straight. Some were blonde, some very dark, others a fiery, almost obnoxious red. Their eyes were every color possible; from greens that matched their trousers to brown so dark you could hardly make out their pupils.

I was about to ask how Burn had become leader of the motley crew when I was accosted by a glittering, giggling, squealing pack. The boys pushed back from the table in a startled huff. Plunder dove under to join them. A whirlwind of girls with hairclips, feathers and shiny bits, surrounded me. In moments, they bedecked me with broken, bent, mismatched pieces of costume jewelry. Knotted bows and ribbons pulled my hair into a pile atop my head.

A blonde girl, caked in too much eye shadow and rouge, mounted the table and propped a large reflective disc before me. From a bag, hung at her waist, she pulled several cracked tubes of cast off cosmetics and a giant makeup brush. I coughed as she shook a great billowing pink cloud over my face. I was offered a moment to gaze at the disturbing image reflected in the old serving platter. I smiled, and as quickly as they had tumbled in the girls were gone. All my years of not being allowed to play dress up made up for in a matter of minutes.

Pillage wrapped her tiny arms around my neck and squealed. "You look beautiful! And now you have treasures to start your hoard." She shook my armful of rattling bangles.

"Tierannie!" A tall, gangly red haired girl sidled up beside me. "Have you thought where you are going to live?"

The rest of the girls, and a handful of nosey boys, hovered in to hear my answer.

"Live?" I shook my head.

"Well, yes, silly," giggled a plump, over made up

blonde around a wad of chewing gum." You have to sleep sometimes. You are more than welcome in our clubhouse." She offered.

I smiled at the thought of living in a house, or more likely a cave, over stuffed with all things girly.

"Well maybe she would rather stay with us?" One of the boys squeaked.

When I looked carefully, I realized she was actually a girl, though not nearly so girly. She had chopped her hair at a ragged angle, and her shirt was the top half of the standard dress. I realized half the faces surrounding me that I had thought were young boys, were really girls.

I giggled.

Debating the two very different households, I was not sure I would fit in either one.

Pillage spoke up. "She is going to guard the Grotto of course! That is her bridge after all!"

"Oh, but won't you get lonely out there?" A pigtailed girl wondered.

I gulped, I had no intention of staying, but they were being so kind, I did not have the heart to say so.

The girls continued to chatter away about living arrangements and drifted off to take seats along the table.

Burn and his boys returned to their antics now that the girls had left. Burn's disgusted scowl at the performance was betrayed by a subtle nod and a wink of approval.

"How old are most of the Trolls?" I looked around the room.

"Old?" Pillage and Plunder giggled.

"It is odd for someone to ask such a question."

Burn seemed equally amused.

"I didn't mean to offend anyone." I shrugged. "I just recall something Pillage and Plunder said."

Pillage's eyes sparkled. She seemed thrilled that I remembered the comment.

"You told the twins to grow up." I prodded Burn. "They said they couldn't."

"Of course they can grow up." Burn shook his head at Pillage and Plunder. "You can have a birthday whenever you like."

"We know." The twins hung their heads a moment.

Then, on second thought, they threw back their bodies in a double reverse roll. "If we did though . . ."

"We couldn't do that." They finished in a split on the floor behind the bench.

Burn rolled his eyes at the performance. He returned his attention to my question at hand. "Birthdays do not come just once a year, and sometimes not for several." Burn's words confused me. "Sometimes, birthdays come all in a matter of days. Trolls are allowed to stay young as long as they like. Until a Troll decides he or she is ready to get another year older, and see life from a different point of view, he or she may stay the same age."

Before I could ask for further clarification, the room filled with the noise of clattering dishes. The mouthwatering aroma that had earlier greeted my senses was accompanied by a delectable symphony of even more treats. Dozens of tiny feet marched up and down between the table rows.

The giant stood with ladle in hand, beside a monstrous stew pot.

I drooled as the children seated around me rose to acquire their dinner. I looked on as older children assisted younger. Some even carried infants, and mashed food into bowls for them.

Pillage took my hand and we ran to form a line where Drake stood. Burn and Plunder hurried up behind us. We worked down the buffet. Baked chicken legs tumbled into properly lumpy mashed potatoes soupy with rich yellow butter. Chocolate cake dripped with strawberry jam. At the center of each pile a tower of fluffy pancakes wobbled, sticky with real maple syrup.

Finally, I sat, the mouth-watering treasure before me.

Pairs of children, carrying a pitcher of bright, sweet smelling, juice, and a tower of wobbling cups, scurried behind benches offering everyone a drink.

I searched for a fork with one hand and a spoon with the other. Looking down at the empty spaces that would be the proper places for the silverware, I sighed. I had no utensils. I peered over the hotcake tower to see Burn take a large scoop from his mashed potatoes—with his hand.

Auntie's voice in my head cursed this barbaric behavior. I looked to either side. I was surrounded by endless rows of children joyously shoveling food into eager mouths. Some even ignored the main course and dove right into the cake.

My tongue traced a smile across my lips as I returned my attention to my plate. I relished the idea of diving right in but, being still new at this wild form of dining, opted to start with the chicken leg. I gripped the joint full-handed and took a greedy bite. My mouth dripped from the tender, juicy meat.

It needed one more thing. I swirled it into the gooey cake topping. Spectacular!

I picked my teeth with a bit of chicken bone and sighed over the empty plate. The swirl of red and yellow and gold on the dish seemed to smile at me. I lifted the plate in both hands and licked the dish clean. I let the plate clatter to the table. Gleefully slamming down the cup drained of tongue tingling juice, I dared to burp, picturing Auntie's horrified expression at such behavior.

The thought shot me to my feet. I wiped my face with my sleeve. Auntie! Mother! They would be terribly worried and angry by now.

The twins dropped their food and stood with me. "What's . . ."

"Wrong. . . ?" they chimed.

Burn looked up too, his mouth full of food.

"I have to get home. Mother will be frantic. This was a lot of fun, but I really must go." I moved to go back the way we had come in.

"You can't go back, Tierannie." Burn leapt over the table and barred my path. "You are one of us now. You were meant to be one of us. Now that you are found, there is no way you can go back."

His eyes quivered with determination and something else.

"But . . ." I could feel my eyes burn.

"Look," he said, "we all want you to stay. Even I want you to stay. But if you are going to cry about it, maybe we can see what the Queen can do. He set a hand on my shoulder. "Besides, time moves different here, remember? They probably don't even know you are missing, yet. Maybe, Up There, you haven't even fallen into the river, yet."

It was a very strange suggestion. Burn patted my seat and slid under the table. With one last longing look at the tunnel to the throne room, I moved back to my place. Anyone who could create the night sky from river rocks could easily get me home without being missed. Still, my excitement had worn off.

"So," Burn asked around a mouthful of chicken, "what's so great about being Up There anyway?"

"Yes . . ." Pillage bounced on the bench.

"You promised . . ." Plunder did the same on the other side.

"To tell us . . ." Their jumping about drew the attention of others nearby.

"All about . . ." Their eyes glittered with curiosity.

"Up There." Faces suddenly turned to me from all sides.

Obviously, the twins were not the only ones who wanted to know.

All of these children were lost, or discarded, and likely knew very little of the world. There were so many of them. I looked into the faces closest to me. Different from my pale round features; their eyes and hair were dark, their bodies very slim and their skin was a yellow gold color. They huddled together like a family. Where had they come from?

I thought about Mother, and where she might have ended up had Auntie not taken her in. I was not sure if I wanted to tell them about all they had missed, or if it was better or worse than what they had here. I was not an authority on any of it, living my life in a sort of prison, as nice as it might have been. Looking at the eager faces though, I had to give them something.

Before I could begin, a terrible din arose from the tunnel. A group of children armored in old tin cans and trash bin lids burst from the darkness, crying and screaming. "The Queen! The Queen is missing!"

The youngest of the children wept. "What do we do? Where can she be?"

Another in the strange armor displayed a square of paper.

Burn leapt across the table, his feet kicking aside plates. He took the note from the teary child. After a long moment, he looked at the others. ""We must take this to Drake."

I followed Burn as he and the others made for the opening at the far end of the cavern. If something had happened to the Queen, what did that mean for me? I didn't want to be selfish, but concern rose through me.

We burst into a large space, heat rippled and the blast of warmth carried all the odors of a busy kitchen. A spiraling network of iron pipes circled the high walls leading to a dark boulder at the center. The boulder at the center of the space belched a column of flame. It shot through the funnel into the ceiling. From the iron labyrinth, hundreds of pots, pans and an array of kitchen utensils dangled. Though moving in haste, I took care not to knock my head on the low hanging items.

My gaze traveled along rows of stools, some occupied by young chefs working at the curving countertop. Pots bubbled at intervals along the outcropping. Holes bored into the smooth surface allowed heat from another ring of glowing red iron to rise through, stoves powered by the system off the central oven.

Amazing. My awe distracted me from the reason I had followed the Trolls into this mad room, until I set eyes on the creator of the ingenious design.

Drake nearly dropped a tray of bread at the sight of the Queen's guards, and the crowd of wailing Trolls.

"What is going on now?" Drake's tone was filled with kindness, but concern washed over his features at the invasion of his kitchens.

"The Queen is gone missing!" Burn shoved the paper at Drake.

This time the bread tray did clatter to the ground.

The giant's spindly legs crumpled beneath him. "Tell me how you know she is missing. Slowly. What did you see? Did she leave any sign of where she could've gone?"

His trembling hand dangled the ragged square of paper before him. He shook his head as he examined the item. His watery eyes stared at the gathered children. "It's a note." He hung his head. "I cannot read."

The children turned to one another. None of them were able to decipher the words. I pushed to the front of the crowd and gently took the paper from the gentle giant.

I was in no way prepared for what I read.

"You will bring to my castle all the keys that open the gates that join the bridges of the surface world, in exchange for your Queen."

I raised my gaze to the crowd. "It's signed, Arakne. Who is she?" Their faces did not reassure me that this was an easy problem. "

Drake began to cry giant blubbering sobs. I had never been as uncomfortable as I was at witnessing a giant weep. Enormous teary blobs flowed down the long slope of his nose and pooled at his knees. The children joined him. Part of me want to too, but when I saw even Burn close to tears I swallowed my fear and stepped up to take control of the situation.

"Why not simply give this Arakne the keys?" I shrugged.

Drake sniffed. "We can't. The witch would use the keys to open the gates between our world and the Up There. She could take over any world she pleased. He wiped at his nose with his sleeve. "Besides, only the Queen knows where all the keys are."

I glanced around at the vast collection of sobbing faces. "But, there are so many of you. Why not just walk right up and get your Queen back?"

The sobbing stopped. After a few stray sniffles the hall became eerily quiet.

Drake wiped his sleeves across his face. "No Troll has ever ventured down the Jungle path to the witch's castle. There is no telling what is out there."

"We are just kids, Tierannie. We are no match for the witch." Burn sighed.

The others nodded in agreement.

Shock and confusion warred within me, but it was anger that won out. I shoved Burn to the ground. "How can you say that? How can you, who severed the head off a giant snake? And, you told me you enjoyed the dangers of the Jungle." Tears trailed my burning cheeks. "How could any of you say such things and expect me to believe it?" I wiped hard at my face with both hands. "She is the only one who can get me back home. You said so."

Burn sat on the ground. He stared wide-eyed at me.

I planted my feet. "Well, I want to go home. I am not going to let some mean old witch stop me. I'll go get the Queen back on my own if I have to." I stomped away. The wall of children parted as I approached.

I did not know what I intended to do. I was deathly afraid of the Jungle after only crossing it once. I knew none of its tricks. I did not even know how to get to the witch's castle. Even if I happened to find it, I had no idea how to fight a witch or rescue a queen. I was not about to spend the rest of my life here though, never having said goodbye to Mother. The Queen of the Trolls was the only one who could help.

I ran through the tunnel. It seemed darker and longer without the smell of baked chicken leading my nose. Without a crowd of children, my lone footsteps echoed in the darkness. I splashed into the lake in the empty throne room. Without the Queen, the moon and stars had fallen. The room had lost all magic. I sloshed through the cold water. A soft glow lit the room from the lakebed. I held my breath and ducked under the chill water. Through the ripples I caught sight of the moon. I retrieved the glowing orb and came up for air. This at least was still blessed with the Queen's magic.

A small hand tapped on each of my shoulders.

"Tierannie," the twins pleaded, "don't go without us."

Burn stood behind them. "Well, if a stupid girl is

not afraid of being cooked and eaten by the witch, then neither am I."

"Eaten?" I flinched.

With a splash, the giant tumbled from the tunnel. "I can't just let you go off on your own, now."

"Told you he had a crush on the Queen," Pillage hissed in my ear.

A wall of faces waited behind Drake. "The rest of you go on and search for the keys. Search everywhere." He waved them off,

The faces disappeared back into the tunnel.

"Do you think they will find all the keys?" Burn stared into the dark after them

"I don't know, Burn, but I certainly hope so." Drake stared after the children, as well.

"Well, there can't be that many places to look." I sloshed toward them. "Couldn't some of them come with us? I mean we are going off to fight a witch. We'll need all the help we can get, don't you think?"

All four raised their eyebrows at me as if I was crazy.

Drake rested a hand on my head. "Believe me, even all those Trolls will have a hard time covering the ground that needs covering."

"You have no idea how big this kingdom is, do you?" Burn stretched out his arms.

I shook my head.

"Big." The twins splashed behind me.

It was the way they said the word that made me realize the true extent of this scavenger hunt. This could take a while.

"What have you got there in your hand, Tierannie?" Drake hovered over the glowing stone in my hand.

"The moon," I offered, "something in me says to take it with us."

I slipped the stone into my apron pocket. The room dimmed into darkness.

We splashed toward the light from the Jungle. One girl, three Trolls, and one giant; the strangest rescue party I had never imagined.

CHAPTER SEVEN:
THE ARMORY, THE KNIGHT, AND THE MASKS

The Jungle seemed even darker than it had on the way into the caves. The path had changed. Instead of one snaking rainbow sand trail, there were three. The footprints appeared in the sand. The path would know which way to go, all we need do was follow our own trail. Pleased with myself for learning so quickly one of the tricks of this world, I waited for prints to appear.

The tracks took two of the three forks. Confused, I looked at Burn. His smug grin and glinting eyes were a sure sign he was more than happy to explain.

"Apparently, we are not all meant to travel the same route." He pointed to the tracks on the left. "See there. Drake and I will travel this way." He indicated to the right. "You see tracks made by you and the twins."

"Well done, Mr. Holmes." I set my hands on my hips. "But why do you suppose we are not all traveling together?"

Burn not only missed the literary reference, he also gaped at me with no further insight.

"That's an easy one." Drake bent to be level with the rest of us. "The reason is because I need to fetch my armor. My house is down that way, and Burn here is my squire. I will need his assistance in suiting up."

"Armor?" The twins chimed.

"Well, yes. I can't very well be a proper knight going off to rescue a damsel in distress without my armor." His shrugging shoulders made it seem silly to consider any other way to proceed.

Drake assured the twins and me that a shortcut near his cave would eventually connect with the path we took. He didn't seem certain where the two roads met, only that they did. The twins appeared to have complete faith in Drake's navigational knowledge of the Jungle, as they saluted briefly and began following their footprints. Burn and I, however, exchanged skeptical glances over our shoulders as we went our separate ways.

The Jungle seemed far less green. I had not before noticed the enveloping quiet or the constricting nature of the space just off the path. Without a clear source of breeze, the whisper of leaves was rare and brief. Now and again my eyes would flit to a slip of movement in the shadows, but when I looked, I could see nothing. Distraction at the newness of the sights and the thought of meeting the Queen had blurred my senses earlier. I considered my Jungle, how frightening the shadows appeared on gloom filled days. In truth, they were completely harmless. Not so here. The darkness here hid things exactly as dangerous as I could fear.

In Burn's absence, our mighty band did not seem so mighty. The twins marched nervously close to one another, their steps void of their usual lightness and bounce. I chose not to voice my own unease. Drake seemed the fatherly sort, if a bit scatterbrained. He would not have left our trio if he thought we could not handle ourselves. I hoped. I stared at another shift in the Jungle branches, and wondered how much he assumed we could fend against.

The twins sang.

My mind kept busy, wondering how a handful of children and a noble giant expected to confront the task at hand. Stalking out of the dining cave, I had not thought about where to go or that anyone would follow. Now that I had more time to consider the task, it felt quite hopeless. I hadn't any weapons with which to fight a witch. I patted my pockets for the rattle stuffed into my apron, the leftover matches, and the river rock moon.

I had no armor like Drake, which I somehow doubted would be much help. I pictured the soup cans with the bottoms cut out that the troll guards clattered through the caves in. This was a fool's errand, but there was no backing out now.

I should have been paying attention to the lyrics of the song the twins sang.

We curved around a sharp bend in the path and the Jungle came to an abrupt halt at another large cavern mouth. This one, much like the throne room, was well lit, though no candles or lamps hung within. The similarities with the Queen's cavern ended with the lighting. Like the Grotto, toys lined walls. The toys here though were highly specified, for war.

Popguns with severed cork strings, wooden swords with edges sanded sharp, BB guns, toy tanks, slingshots with artillery consisting of pickup sticks and jacks, wagons laden with crates and covered with trash cans, bicycles and tricycles armed and armored, sacks of water balloons tied to jars sticky with syrups and jams, marbles that could be ammunition for any of the trajectory weapons, an array of bent and broken silverware, and eggs that looked as if they had been rotting since the twins were infants. An endless arsenal of doodads and what-have-yous. All made to look deadlier than they probably were, but meant to make you wonder only after you turned tail and headed for the proverbial hills. At last, in the silence of my awe, I heard the song the twins sang:

"The trolls march in and the trolls march out,
Beneath the bridges hear them shout.
They play their drums, make lots of noise.
They make weapons out of toys."

Still singing, the duo scrambled into the room, loading a wagon-tank, scurrying from shelf to alcove and handing off weapons. I joined the dance. Toward the rear of the room, the twins paused the loading process to stand in the center of piles of pots, pans, soup cans, trashcan lid shields, helmets, and colanders. The twins assisted one another, sliding cans over elbows and knees, linking shoe laces through holes, adjusting gloves and colander helmets. Daring to help myself to the armor, I ducked my head between a pair of trash lids and adjusted the leather shoulder straps. Pillage and Plunder each took a side and tied off the laces with sloppy bows. Satisfied with my appearance only after settling a large pot on to my head, the twins scurried to an enormous curtained wall at the rear of the cavern.

Each in turn hauled on the thick braided rope running through the vast pulley system arching overhead. They stretched and heaved and the curtain lurched folding to one side. As the fabric ebbed, a gruesome, twisted array of faces sent shivers down my spine.

Masks. Dozens of them. Each hand-made caricature dripped with bead and findings, glittering with ferocious beauty. As unique as the children I had met at dinner.

The twins rolled a ladder from behind the lumpy curtain folds and, in turn, scurried up the rungs to retrieve their faces. Pillage's pale, rosy-cheeked mask was encrusted with glittering bits of broken costume jewelry. A mane of pearls clicked and rattled down her back as she shook her head with mock ferocity. Plunder's lacked the pearly tendrils, but not the black sparkle of treasures. A Jolly Roger sneered from each cheek, peering over a rattling beard of gold coins that rang with every fearsome hop he took. As they shook their sibling faces that matched like Comedy and Tragedy, I offered a respectable tremble.

A brief ripple of jealousy followed the duo as they turned away and pranced to the wall, growling and yipping.

"Burn helped us . . ." Plunder pivoted.

"Make this . . ." Pillage twirled to his side.

"After you . . ." The two parted.

"Escaped to the . . ." They held a third mask between them.

"Up There!" They bubbled with mirth behind their masks.

"He was quite sure . . ." Together they held the piece to me.

"You would come back." They set it in my waiting palms.

Trembling, I closed my fingers around the edges of the prize. The blue green bits mosaicked over the surface seemed priceless treasures, though to the untrained eye they might appear as broken odds and ends. I petted the silken peacock feathers that sprung at all angles across the brow and traced the intricate bends in the golden, Greek-key border that gashed beneath one eye and over the bridge of the nose, trailing my fingers down its path to the base of the cheek. Between two thick, red lips hung a pair of long, serrated, fangs of gold that gave a believable illusion of sharpness. Pearls clung in tiers along the forehead.

Tearing my gaze away, I looked to Pillage and saw random gaps in her pearly tresses.

She dragged a toe through the dirt and a hand through the strands. "Makes us match."

"Thank you." Flooded with joy and excitement as I ran a finger over the fangs, I breathed again. "It is the most beautifully terrifying thing I have ever seen."

The twins tackled me in a joyous embrace and helped affix my new face. I fought my frizzing, wild curls—still adorned with a chaos of ribbons and hair clips—to hug the edges of the mask.

"Perfectly . . ." Pillage tied off the bow.

"Horrible . . ." Plunder nodded his approval.

Into our tank, we packed five of each firearm, and most of the ammunition, and somehow hauled it out of the armory. The twins groaned against the pull of the handle with all their might, armor clanking. My heels dug into the graveled floor as I shoved the cart on to the path.

Fully armed, but still worried, the idea that we might have a chance seemed to grow. Having everything we could need to throw at an enemy did diminish fears of what lurked in the Jungle. Let anything dare cross three frightening trolls.

The twins and I drove along the sandy path, following our footprints and made a game of trying to trick them. In turn, we hopped onto the wagon, watched the pattern shift and jumped off again. I applauded the twins' dances while watching the sands run about. It seemed to mimic a choreography of tiny beetles as I walked on my hands.

Having such a wonderful time, no one asked are we there yet. Part of my mind did toy with the thought that if we never wanted the journey to end, maybe it never would. This worried me, but arriving at the Witch's castle without Drake or Burn concerned me more. I kept the thought confined to my mind.

"So." I walked on my hands again to turn my thoughts to other things. "This witch, what sorts of magic does she use?"

"Oh, no." Pillage's feet skipped beside me.

"Arakne hates . . ." Plunder grunted against the weight of the wagon.

"Magic," the pair finished as Plunder moved to assist with the wagon again.

I tumbled onto my rear, directly onto the newly-formed, round print, blocking the path. "But, if she doesn't use magic, what makes her a witch?"

They shivered. "She's mean."

Of course. The Queen of the Trolls is a beautiful sorceress, giants are kindly cooks, trolls are lost children. Why would a witch be more than a mean old woman? All the fairy tales were completely off the mark.

I fell into hysterics in the middle of the road.

"What?" Indigence from the twins struck me in full duplex.

"Well." I sighed relief through my laughter. "If Arakne has no magic and the Queen does, why do we need to rescue her?"

"Because . . . " The twins' sigh was not one of relief.

"Arakne drains power . . ." Their masks knocked together.

"Leaving no magic at all." Their tiny bodies sagged to the ground.

They slumped together on the path. My giggles were swallowed by their sorrow. I clanked across the short space to encircle them in my arms.

"I'm sorry," I whispered into the hollow between their faces. "I didn't understand. We will save her." I squeezed them. "I promise."

"Ugh," a voice of disgust called out. "What is this sob story?"

I grabbed a loaded popgun from the edge of the wagon and spun to aim at the potential foe.

Towering before me stood a crooked, rust

patched, armored knight. Atop this giant, perched a small silver being with a flame-colored face and razor-toothed gold grin.

The twins tumbled and banged from behind me. "Burn!"

"Drake!" They howled and wrapped around the giant's rusty armored legs.

Drake tipped back his visor as he bent to his knees. The movement was too much for Burn. Though he scrambled to keep his perch, his tin canned form scraped and bumped down the giant's back. Drake swung an arm to catch him, but it did no good.

Burn landed at my feet with a clatter.

"Good form." I grinned through my mask at Burn's dented soup can chest plate. "Was that meant to be a swan dive or an albatross?"

"Glad to have us all together again." Burn grumbled and clanked as he righted himself and adjusted the cans on his arms.

"Nice face." I brushed past to inspect Drake, surprised to find the giant's armor real, ancient and in poor repair, but nonetheless real.

Hands crossed over the pommel of his sword, Drake struck a noble pose. I circled his gangly form and tapped the suit. The rust coating the surface stole the shine from the otherwise clearly noble knight.

Gentle hands pried the twins from Drake's legs then moved to take hold of the wagon handle. "Well done." He inspected the pint-sized tank and inventoried the arsenal.

I was fairly certain he was as clueless as the rest of us as to what we needed to take down Arakne. I remained silent, though, as he checked the sights on popguns, the stretch of slings and the heft of the balloons.

He arranged the weapons back inside the wagon, then straightened and lashed a vine to the handle. "Okay, Trolls. Forward, march."

With Drake towing the tank, the going eased. Pillage and Plunder marched in the lead, their little knees lifting high. Burn and I held the rear and picked and collected, spilled balloons and displaced jacks from the path. Our march continued in measured silence for a stretch before Drake decided to mention the first of the many perils on the road to the witch's castle—The Dread Dot.

CHAPTER EIGHT:
THE DREAD DOT, THE MUSES, AND
THE BALLERINA

"The Dread Dot?" I stopped the tank with a tug. "What is that?"

Drake lifted his faceplate. "If you'll not jerk the tank so and make me lose my train of thought." He winked and continued his march at a slightly slower pace. "Between here and the witch's castle, stands the Hall of the Muses. The hall was once something of legend among Trolls. Within its alcoves, great works were displayed. When the witch came, bent on destruction of all that is free, and wild, and creative in the Jungle, she brought with her a fiercely mundane creature. It grew, and grew, feeding off the art in the hall, becoming something no troll could overcome.

"The Dot takes up a full wall in the entryway." Burn cut in. "It forces all the real art to skulk about in corners."

"That is why . . ." Pillage stroked the pearl tendrils of her mask.

"We put so much work . . . " Plunder touched the cheeks of the Jolly Rogers.

"Into our masks." The pair trembled.

"There is no other way to feed the muses in the Jungle that wander aimless, weary in their search for an artist." Burn nodded.

"What about in the hall?" I clenched the edge of my mask.

"No one knows." Drake sent an audible rattle shuddering through his armor. "The most common guess is they are allies to the witch."

I considered this sordid tale a moment. "Wait. It is just a dot right?"

An exchange of glances and a communal nod confirmed my guess.

"Well, then maybe someone should just stand up to it. Take it down. Tell it outright that it isn't really art at all. Put it in its place." I drove my fist into my palm.

Burn gestured up the trail. "Here's your chance."

There. In the center of the path, completely blocking our passage, stood a set of massive marble steps beyond a row of ivory columns. Between the centermost pillars shone a glint of glass double doors with tarnished handles. This gothic building grew down from the roof of the caverns in a seamless transition from the stalactites and stretched across the width of the tunnel.

"You would do that?" Drake fell to one knee before me.

"Do what?" I stepped away. "What? No! No, not me." I tumbled over the handle of the tank as I backed. "What I meant was someone." Past Drake's face, Pillage and Plunder's eyes glistened at me. "Not me."

The eerily quiet hall swallowed my attention. The building was not the least bit inviting, even without the story of The Dot.

"I didn't mean me." I spoke as if the pillars might listen.

"Of course, you didn't mean you." Burn clapped a hand on my shoulder.

I flinched.

"There is no way you would be able to face off against The Dread Dot." With both hands on my shoulders, he spoke into my ear. "I mean. You are just a girl. And human. Look." He turned me to face the twins and Drake again. "Pillage here has been a troll far longer than you and she is terrified of The Dot." He crossed between the others and me. "No one expects you to be brave enough for this."

The twins pushed Burn aside. "Yes, we do."

Burn shoved them away with an irritated glare.

"Just a girl, huh?." I dug a slingshot and a water balloon bomb from the tank. "I am just as troll as the rest of you. In fact." I shook the syrupy orb in Burn's face. "I am probably more so!" I snapped tight the knot on the balloon to make my point.

My frustration pushed me to the base of the steps. Then, I froze. I swallowed hard and my pride thumped the butterflies in my stomach.

"Oh, go on." I jumped as Burn nudged my shoulder. "Not like we would make you go alone."

Relief swept over me as I took in the armed quartet.

Our army of five stalked shoulder to shoulder up the marble steps. Armor and cans rasped and rattled with every step, though we hoped for stealth there was little we could do to quiet our trembling knees. I held my syrup balloon low and my slingshot high. Whatever lay behind that door, I was ready.

A sidelong glance around the team confirmed their preparedness. Burn hefted a balloon in each hand like grenades. Pillage and Plunder crouched either side of Burn, popguns loaded with spiked corks. Drake brought up the rear, crouched as best his gangly form allowed, his club held high.

Burn held his hand up when we reached the doorway. He placed a finger to the lips of his mask, then tilted his head.

Burn and pillage ducked off to one side while Pillage and I scooted to the other. Drake took center.

Burn nodded his head, once . . . twice . . . thrice!

With the form of a professional baseball player, Drake swung his club against the doors. The glass shattered as the doorframes flew from their hinges.

Four trolls tumbled into the main room of the hall, whooping, yelling, and shooting in every direction.

"Stop!" Balloons and corks sailed around me. "Stop!"

Burn and the twins ceased their howls and lowered their weapons.

Drake's rampant hollers echoed off the otherwise silent walls. Burn poked him between the joints of his armor, offering a subtle shake of his head. Drake fell silent as he rubbed at his side.

The foyer walls were bare along either side. In place of paintings, bright squares patched the faded walls. Blobs of syrup dripped in the arched alcoves. On the wall opposite the entrance, I saw it.

A huge white canvas occupied the entirety of the

wall, at the center a large, red, perfectly round, smooth edged circle—The Dread Dot.

Squinting, I tipped back my mask and approached with careful, yet determined steps.

"This," I scoffed as I turned on my heel and raised an eyebrow. "This is your terrifying piece of non-art." I jabbed a critical finger at the canvas.

"Shh!" The others hissed and waved to silence me.

"What?" I stared. "It's only a dumb circle on a boring white space. It's not like it's going to jump off the wall and come after us." The reek of oil paints began to mix with the sweetness of the syrup. "Let's just take it down."

Still the others gaped and waved at me.

Slowly, I turned to yank down the boring image. My shoulder thumped against a wall of red, tacky with oil paints. I inhaled an acrid odor mixed of turpentine, paint, and mildewed cloth. I tilted my head as far back as I could to find the edge, but Dots do not have edges. The Dot seemed to exhale a rank breath of spoiled acrylics.

I patted my pockets to retrieve a broken jack. Point blank I fired from my slingshot. It pinged off the surface. I held my breath as I listened to the projectile skitter across the smooth floor.

The Dot did not flinch. Could Dots flinch?

"That's not good, is it?" I leaned only a hair closer to the others. I coughed.

"Not good at all!" Burn had Pillage and Plunder by the hand.

Drake snatched hold of my collar and hauled me backwards around a corner. Burn and the twins followed close behind. I flailed and called out cues to duck and shoot. What had been a harmless dot had sprouted stick arms and legs.

It looked more like art that way, but I was very critical about artwork that wanted to devour me.

It had no face, so the worst it could do was tear us to shreds with its needle-like fingers. Drake slid around into another room. The Hall of Muses was even larger than it appeared from the outside. The layout of the galleries twisted in a labyrinth of rooms and alcoves. We dove, and skidded into a dark room. Drake yanked the others in as they passed the entryway

We huddled in the shadowed walls, holding our breath. The Dot thundered past.

"This is ridiculous." I thumped back against the wall. "We are running from a drawing."

"A very angry drawing." Burn shook my shoulders.

"I'm not ashamed to be running from it." Drake's knees trembled.

The twins' masks rattled as they nodded.

"Well, we can't hide out here forever." I straightened.

"We have," a chorus of whispers echoed from the darkness.

Armor clattered again.

Sallow faces, five in all, emerged from the wall of the alcove. Ghosts from ancient Greece. Both men were bald and the women had hair stacked in curls and tendrils upon their heads. Their cheekbones spiked out below sandbagged eyes. Long white robes flowed from the wall as they floated into our space. A collective shiver coursed through our band.

Running seemed like a good idea, except for the menace of facing the Dot again.

"Do not be afraid," the first spirit yawned. "We are allies in a common fear."

A female spirit straightened her back. "We are the muses, trapped by The Dread Dot."

"What masterpieces you wear upon your heads." A second female caressed the pearly tendrils of Pillage's mask.

Pillage swallowed, but did not move away.

A blush of color rose to the Muse's pale cheeks, a shadow of former beauty that might have inspired poetry or paintings.

The other Muses echoed her movement as they reached to stroke masks and armor with ghostly fingertips.

As my fear slipped away, a desire to be rid of the Dot rose in its place.

Burn jumped. His sudden movement scattered the spirits to the safety of the walls.

"I have an idea!" His words drew the Muses out again. "As we were running through the galleries, I noticed a door behind the place where the Dot was hanging."

"Are you certain?" A Muse appeared beside Burn's head.

His startled shiver a fair payback. Burn nodded.

Drawing the circle close with a wave of his hands, all ears turned to Burn, as he explained his plan.

"I couldn't think why The Dot would be hung in front of a door. Then I realized," Burn's smile crooked as he looked to the Muses for assurance. "The missing artwork has to be somewhere."

"That is fine." I shrugged. "But what good does it do? How will it help defeat the Dot?"

"It will help us." The oldest looking Muse tugged at his long beard in thought. "And in turn we will be able to help you."

"Okay." Drake nodded, his visor dropping forward. Lifting it back into place. "What's the plan?"

Burn led the way to the main gallery, scouting around each turn as we moved through the rooms. Scooting to a wall opposite Drake, Pillage, Plunder and I, the Muses floated into position beside us.

We stared at the door Burn had discovered.

No sign of the Dot.

"Go." I waved him on. "Get it open. We'll cover your back. " My whispers felt too loud in my ears.

Burn darted to the door. He faltered with the doorknob a moment then turned with a shrug.

"Do not despair." The bearded Muse set his hand on the crown of my mask. "We will manage the lock."

"We have regained much strength from your beautiful masks." One of the women ran her fingers through the pearls of Pillage's mask.

Across the open floor, past a quizzically staring Burn, and into the keyhole, the Muses slipped.

The moments that passed remained silent enough that the click of the lock carried across the gallery.

Muses bubbled back out of the keyhole one-by-one and hovered beside the door.

A last scan around the room, and Burn turned the large brass knob with both hands. I winced as the door creaked open. The space beyond was black.

Burn turned to us. Uncertainty battled to overtake the brave face he offered.

I patted my apron pockets, recalling the supplies still wrapped tight inside the beret. I drew the matches from the folds, thankful they were still dry after so many swims. The little book hissed over the floor to rest against Burn's toes. Picking a match from the pack, he gifted me with a smile. the first one genuine of pride he had given me. Then, he disappeared into the darkness.

I held my breath, and felt certain the others did as well.

"What if the Dot is in there?" Plunder squeezed my hand.

"What if nothing is in there?" Pillage took the other.

In answer, an orange glow flickered into life beyond the door, followed by another, and a third. The white edge of a canvas scraped across the threshold revealing a glorious, vivid splatter painting of butterflies in flight. Burn pushed from behind it.

Released from our worry a collective sigh escaped into the silence.

Burn puffed his chest and jutted both thumbs into the air. This act caused the painting to clatter to the floor.

"Shhh!" We hissed.

Burn grinned. At least he had the sense to appear sheepish. He righted the painting and beckoned us to join him, before he disappeared back into the hidden room.

We scurried after him. Tumbling over one another we surveyed the enormous space alighted by a few deeply melted, lumpy candles. The priceless contents inside the room filled our nostrils with the scent of paint, glue, chalk, and wax.

Stacks of canvas leaned against the walls. Shelves bowed, heavy with colorful sculpture. Volumes of dusty books and scrolls jutted from boxes on the floor. We stood in the treasure hold for every refrigerator masterpiece ever made.

"Stop gawking, start moving." Burn grabbed another canvas, this one a beautiful stick figure ballerina. It reminded me of my arithmetic pencil.

We relayed the paintings to the open light of the gallery. Once we had a handful of artwork installed, the Muses regained enough solidity to assist in the shuffle. The room bustled with movement and color. Burn, Pillage, Plunder and I set to work placing images along the walls of the front gallery. Drake followed, hanging each piece on a high nail.

Muses danced about the room touching each coloring in the pieces. As they did so, a smear of color absorbed into their pale bodies. At first, they looked like granite statues spattered in random paints. Yet, the more frames hung and sculptures were set upon pedestals, the less patched their color became. The balding men's great snowy beards grew warm with rich reds and browns. Theirs heads shone muted tones in tan and peach. The women's hair, once grey, glowed blonde, black and brown. Their skin, young and vibrant, reflected golden brown.

Now, I could see the inspiration.

With a shuddering bang, attention flew from the Muses' transformation to the door. We had failed to keep watch.

The huge, red Dot had resumed its place before

the door. We froze. It stared, without eyes, gauging which of us to take out first.

Without a moment to think, I threw open a nearby book and read aloud the first thing I could. A child's poem to his mother. It wasn't Shakespeare, but it was a work of art.

The Dot tore at non-existent ears.

I flipped to another page. A story about a beloved bunny.

The Dot raged, flailing its stick like arms

A Muse handed each twin a crayon, one green, one blue. The twins didn't need to be told what to do. They lunged at the distracted Dot and scrawled across the plain red surface.

The scribbles twisted into a pain-crumpled face. The Dot howled with its newly formed mouth. Tears bloomed from the corners of its lopsided, squinting eyes. Burn, in a creative frenzy, drew his dagger, climbed the spindly arms of the Dot, and slashed the smooth arc of the Dot into a wild fringe of hair. The Dot pulled at this with its stick fingers.

I leafed through the book. I paused on a page with only one line. A wish. A childish request from a secret admirer. It was exactly what we needed.

"Will you be my friend?" I read loud and clear over the din of the Dot's howls.

Silence.

I looked up from the book. Where the Dot had been the others stood in an enclosed a circle.

I read the autograph on the note, "Love, Trevor." I closed the book and set it on a nearby pedestal, and hurried to the others.

"You have to teach me how to do that." Burn looked over his shoulder.

I pushed my way between Burn and the blonde Muse. "Do what?"

There, in a ring of feet, lay a large, red paper circle, with a scribbled face, wild, fringed hair and pipe cleaner limbs.

"That." Burn sighed in awe.

"All I did was read the page." I shrugged.

"All of you did this," The Muse who first greeted us, picked up the paper monster's remains, "All of you should take this wonderful work of art home to show your mother.

"Mother!" I suddenly remembered my reason for being out here in the first place.

"The Queen!" cried the others.

"Is it true then?" She clasped her beautiful hands in distress. "The Queen of the Trolls has been taken by the Witch Arakne?"

"How did you know?" Burn's brow knit.

"Word travels fast through this part of the jungle." The raven-haired muse leaned down to Burn.

"Rumor has begun that Arakne intends to drain the Queen of magic, then the witch will be the only one capable of using the keys," the bearded Muse said.

"Please . . ." Drake bowed before the Muses. "Tell us the way through to the other side of the Hall of Muses."

"For rescuing us from the terrible reign of The Dread Dot, we will be your guides." The auburn-haired muse held out a hand.

Drake hurried back out the front doors and hauled the loaded tank into the foyer.

Meanwhile, I sighed at the sight of the many

creative works we had hung. My eyes swam in the colors that graced the walls. It was a vibrant contrast to the pale walls seen on our arrival. Peering at a particularly realistic bust of a slightly chubby faced female, I jumped back as it blinked at me and smiled.

"Emily?" A Muse in a pale lime toga hopped from behind the pedestal.

"Yes." I blinked, confused, "I am Emily."

This Muse was the first person in this world to refer to me by that name.

The Muse crouched to her knees, her toga billowing around her.

Her apple cheeks blossomed with color. "Oh! Emily!" Her eyes were welling. "Don't you know me?"

I didn't. She looked as though she might cry, as I stood silent. I had no idea what to do.

Pillage appeared at my side, stomping her little feet with glee. "Oh! Another Muse!"

Pillage's enthusiasm seemed to lighten the Muse's spirit. "I am not just any Muse." She bent into a curtsey. "I belong to Emily."

"Tierannie! You are so lucky!" Plunder was at my arm.

"I am?" I adjusted my mask.

"Of course." Burn marched over to our growing gathering. "You would have your very own Muse."

"I thought Muses inspired everyone." I was not looking for another reason for Burn to dislike me.

"Oh! We do!" My Muse waved her hands. "But truly wonderful artists can claim a Muse of their own." She blushed as she gushed about great artists.

Drake set his hand on Burn's mop of hair.

"Muses can only be mastered by those who dwell Up There."

Drake's words made some sense.

"But, I am only eight." I looked from Drake to the Muse. "How can I be a great artist?"

From the folds of her toga, my Muse retrieved a newly sharpened pencil. "Show them." She offered me the tool. "Show them how we make her dance."

I shook my head, very confused.

"How does one make a pencil dance?" Burn huffed and crossed his arms.

Scowling at him, I realized the meaning. In my Jungle, during lessons, the way I imagined my pencils as ballerinas to pass the time.

"I can only do numbers and letters." I sighed, staring at the yellow stick of wood and lead.

"Not here." My Muse took my shoulders in her soft hands. "Here she can dance."

She stepped in line with the other Muses who gathered to guide us through the Hall. "Go on ahead." She urged me on with her palms up.

The group gathered behind me as I stared at the pencil. I glanced at their faces, then at the plain white floor of the Hall of the Muses. I lowered to one knee at a time and set my right hand on the cool, smooth surface. I gripped the pencil upright in my left hand.

The tip of the lead scratched a slow arc. I drew a circle as neatly as I could. I sat back and nodded to the Trolls and Muses hovering over me. I had no idea what to create.

"Just let her go." Another Muse rested a warm hand on my shoulder. "She will lead the way."

I wrinkled my eyebrows and tilted my head.

Placing the tip back against the floor, I tried again to think. The pencil twitched as I curved an awkward eight. I squinted at the thing as if it might do something. In my moment of absent-mindedness, I loosened my grip.

It leapt from my hand and scrawled the last math problem I had solved before my adventure began, 'Eight plus ten equals'. The Pencil twirled for a moment as it finished the curve of the eighteen. I thought another problem. The Pencil leapt to a clear space on the floor and scrawled the new sequence. I had answered that one wrong. No one seemed to notice.

Three more math problems and a long, completely misspelled word flowed from my mind and carried our path forward. The Pencil took off around the remaining space at the center of the foyer. My mind raced with steps for my dancer to perform. She jumped and twirled, glided and turned spirals. Her dance floor quickly filled with random scrawling, following her movements. Our crowd moved to stay atop the growing images. I found myself dancing right along with the Pencil ballerina.

I spun and dipped and jumped along, just a step behind. The crowd followed through the passage and we left a trail of scribbling in our wake as we traversed the galleries.

The deeper we traveled into the Hall, the more we saw changes wrought by the defeat of The Dot. More and more Muses milled about decorating the walls and stocking the galleries. No more were we faced with bare, yellowed walls and empty pedestals. Works of great art from artists of every age were hung and arranged in every room and hallway.

We twisted and turned our way right to the exit on the other side of the Hall of the Muses. As much as I knew we had to be on our way, by the time we reached the exit, I did not really want to leave.

I paused at the double doors.

The ballerina clattered to the floor, only a nub.

My chest heaving from exercising my creativity, I turned a glowing smile to the group that followed us. Pillage, Plunder, even Burn and Drake busied with crayons, filing color into the markings, making an artistic rendition of the Path to show the way through the hall.

My Muse stepped around the group and dipped to retrieve the pencil from the be-scribbled floor. She smiled at me.

"I told you. You are a real artist." She set the nub in my open palm. "Visit me again as soon as you can. There are many more galleries yet to carpet."

I stared at the bit of pencil in my hand, wonder pausing me before I curled my fingers around it and tucked it into my apron pocket.

Drake and the Trolls rose from their coloring.

The Muses hugged each of us in turn and stood in the open doorway to bid us farewell.

We flowed from the doors and returned to the path. I glanced back only a moment to smile at the dancing green-grey of my Muse's eyes.

"Oh!" A thought jumped into my mind, and I scrambled back to the steps. "Do you have a name?"

My Muse's face bubbled into the biggest grin I had ever seen anyone possess. She threw her arms out as she hurried down the stairs. I could feel my ribs giving in her awesome bear hug. I nearly suffocated in her bosom.

"Carmen." She sang out. "My name is Carmen."

Carmen set me on my feet and I stumbled a bit as air returned to my lungs. "Carmen."

"Tierannie!" Burn's voice echoed across the cavern. "Come on!"

As we entered the Jungle, the path crowded with sandal-shod prints heading toward the Hall. Muses from the Jungle would be close behind, returning to their home.

With a final glance, we resumed our original formation. The witch's castle awaited.

CHAPTER NINE:
PISKIES, DRAGONS, AND TROLLS

We stood in shadows a long while, not speaking, barely breathing - only listening.

"Why did we stop?" I whispered because it seemed appropriate.

"Because the tracks stopped." Drake set down the handle of the wagon and removed his helmet.

He shook his shaggy, brown locks until they returned to pre-helmeted fullness. The twins followed suit, tossing their helmets and masks on top of the tank.

"What? Are we just going to sit here?" I tipped up my mask. "Didn't you hear what the Muses said about the magic?"

"If the path says stop, we have to stop." Burn removed his helmet and mask, wiping his sleeve across his face.

"But, what are we waiting for?" My hands fell to my sides.

"For the path to say go." Drake sat and settled his long legs across the width of the path.

There were no marks showing he would do so. I circled the group, but left no trace. I stepped over Drake's legs and crouched to inspect the path ahead. "Burn," I called over my shoulder.

I lowered my face to within inches of the fine sands. "What sort of markings do you suppose these are?"

Sand crunched beside me as Burn leaned forward. He squinted in the fading light. He moved in for a closer look and nearly fell over, catching himself with his right hand. A left hand print appeared beside it.

Though very small, there were a great many delicate swirls clustered in the sand.

Burn's eyes grew wide. He placed his left palm on the mark and a footprint took shape. In a blink, he leaped over Drake's legs. "Piskies!" He snatched up his mask and helmet and mined the tank for a weapon.

The others shot into action. Drake struggled to get his unwieldy limbs beneath him. In a flash, all four were suited and armed. I followed their lead in panicked confusion.

"Piskies?" I stood beside Burn, near the tank. "What are Piskies? And why are we all excited about them?"

"Piskies are the only things that can confuse the path." Burn lowered his voice and crouched. "And, they are bad news." He tossed me a popgun.

"They confuse travelers, then ambush them." Drake swallowed loudly as he leveled his club.

As if in response, the Jungle suddenly sparked with wild flares. They zipped and zoomed in crazed patterns.

"Guard the tank!" Burn's voice boomed.

I did not argue.

We tightened the circle and prepared for attack.

Killer fairies! I was beginning to wonder where fairytales got their information. Nothing here was according to the books.

The buzzing sparks became less erratic and took on a formidable formation surrounding us. A glowing ring circled above. Light as bright as day closed in around us.

Burn fired a pickup stick spiked cork from his popgun. It whizzed toward the lights, nailing one to a vine. The glow faded to reveal a tiny winged person. The ring stopped spinning a moment, as the Piskies inspected their fallen comrade. With an angry hum the ring whirled and lowered, choking our shrinking space. The attack began. Streaks of kamikaze lights dove for the tank.

One by one, we shot them down, but more rained in.

"What do they want?" I screamed over the hum and fired a syrupy balloon, taking out a section of whirring bodies.

I couldn't yet bring myself to use the makeshift darts, but the syrup glued the wriggling beasts to branches and leaves.

"It's not us they want!" Drake swung his club and a row of Piskies splattered against it.

"It's the tank . . ." Pillage raised a dented trashcan lid and a dozen tiny dents appeared upon its surface.

"And our stuff!" Plunder held a second lid. A flurry of lights pelted it like bugs striking a windshield.

The twins shook off the mangled bodies.

"They steal everything!" Burn fired a barrage of spiked corks. "Rotten little pirates is what they are!" The darts whizzed through the thick of the ring.

I watched in awe as every shot pinned a fading glow to the vines beyond.

Pillage screeched behind me. A band of Piskies hauled at her mask's pearly hair, dragging Pillage along with it.

Tossing my weapon aside, diving to assist her, I cupped the closest ball of light in my hands and yanked it from the pearls. A stab shot through the flesh of my captive's cell. I slammed my palms together. A sticky mass of squished Piskie oozed around a pin-sized sword. "The evil creature stabbed me!" Pity for the little monsters was gone.

Digging into the tank I drew forth a pair of cymbals. I crashed the discs together, smashing the Piskie lighted pearls. For a moment, I held thunder and lightning in my hands. The light flickered out between the cymbals. A dozen tiny bodies rained onto the ground.

"All right! Who's next?" I clapped the cymbals again.

Even with five of us taking down a dozen Piskies with each volley, they still outnumbered us. And showed no sign of giving up without claiming their spoils. My arms ached. There was no way out and apparently no way to win.

A sudden blaze exploded in and orange sweep that tunneled through the jungle vines. Burning Piskies shot off like Fourth of July fireworks.

Before we could react, the remaining Piskies recovered, though they were forced to spread their ring thin to hold formation. We flew back into the fray with renewed energy.

Another bright fireball bowled through their ranks. I ducked as the blast of heat blackened the tips of my feathers.

Beyond the glowing ring of Piskies, two great red eyes blazed from within the vines. The ground shook and the huge head of a black-scaled dragon burst through the branches onto the path.

I dove to the safety of the tank. "Dragon!" I pointed at the head, and most of a long neck, blocking the way.

"Well," Drake groaned, "this can't get much worse, can it?"

"Damned hoard robbers!" the beast howled.

Jagged rows of fangs glowed with the heat of another fireball. We hit the dirt as another blast rippled the air.

Burn shifted in the dirt. "Do you think he is aiming at us or the Piskies?"

"I don't think he really cares." I ducked under the flames of another attack.

A sizzling Piskie fell from the air, landing inches from my nose. Another joined it, and then another, and another. The path became speckled with charred Piskies.

The twins leaped to their feet and ran to the tank. The rain of burned Piskies had set the wood and supplies ablaze. We fought to squelch the fire, crashing cymbals and trash lids over the flames while Burn and Drake scooped sand onto the tank.

Once the fire was out, we swept the sand and charred remains off the tank. Then, we rifled through the mess to assess the damage. Stinking bits of melted balloon clung to blackened jars. The heat had burst some of the glass, leaving rivers and pools of baked syrup spattered on everything nearby. Only a popgun and a handful of ammunition remained.

A disaster.

I sagged against the wagon, smearing charcoal down my back. Our ally of the moment, the dragon, emerged from the Jungle. Its scales shimmered black, red eyes gleamed. The dragon focused on a light that strobed angrily in its talons.

"Where is it?" Flames flicked at each syllable. "Where did you little demons hide my harness?"

The Piskie bit, kicked, and stabbed at the dragon's talons. It showed no sign of cooperation.

"Fine," he snorted. "I'll follow the trail your little band made right back to your dirty hive." Talons sliced together like scissors.

The glow went out.

The beast thumped in our direction, stopping at the wagon to stretch his neck to full length. His talons churned the earth of the path. Looking over the destruction of our arsenal, the monster offered a sigh. "I'm sorry about your toys." He paused as if listening to something. "Thank you for stalling the Piskies. Now, move!" he barked.

We scrambled to obey. The path was barely wide enough for the dragon alone. I glanced down to check my footing. The wheeled tracks of the tank slid into the Jungle, our footprints were nowhere to be found. The path was back to normal, but this did not ease my mind.

The dragon's sigh returned. "Fine," he growled, shifting one large red eye on us. "Get on, but you are going to help me."

We exchanged glances. I hoped the others could make sense of this strange offer. None appeared to have a clue how to approach to the situation.

"Look . . ." The word roared from the dragon's throat.

We started at the din.

"The nagging little voice in my head says I am obliged to take you along. So, get on already. Who knows what those vile little pirates did with my harness. If I don't get it back, believe me, I will never hear the end of it."

A shuffle of feet on sand was all we managed.

"Do I need to resort to threats?" The cool tone stirred us more than any roar.

One by one, Drake lifted us onto the dragon's neck, then vaulted himself up last, settling between the tightly folded wings.

With a sweep of his serpentine tail, the dragon slapped the wagon into the tangles of the Jungle.

In front of me, the twins cringed.

"My name is Easalle." The dragon thundered along the path. " I don't enjoy talking to humans as a rule, but the voice insists I introduce myself."

I was elected via a series of nudges to speak on the group's behalf. "It's very nice to meet you. Mr. Easalle." I swallowed the growing lump in my throat. "My name is Em—ah, Tierannie. My friends . . ." I paused considering for a moment if I had ever used the word out loud before, ". . . are Pillage, Plunder, Burn and Drake. We are Trolls. Well," I corrected, "Pillage, Plunder, Burn and I are. Drake is a giant." Inside my gloves, my hands grew clammy.

Easalle swung his head enough for us to see the

sneer. "I know what you are and I know what you aren't." He rolled his eyes. "Those masks may fool the stupid humans upstairs, but they don't do a thing for me. You are children. Human children." Easalle's back rippled. "I have a load of bad history with humans, so drop the charade at least until we part ways."

Pillage and Plunder slumped in front of me. I thought I heard a sniffle.

"Well, I am no child." Drake straightened on the dragon's back.

"Whatever, chicken legs. Just don't pinch the wings," Easalle hissed back.

After the awkward introductions, none dared speak to the dragon for a long while.

"Excuse me, Dragon." Burn's boredom finally forced him to break the silence.

"Easalle," I corrected.

"Whatever." Burn scowled over his shoulder. "Where are we going? And, why are you even in the Jungle in the first place?"

"No talking." Then, Easalle sighed. "I was searching for the entrance to the Island of Windfall. Rumor has it there is a form of magic there that can help solve a little problem I have been carrying around for quite some time.

"What sort of problem could a dragon have?" Burn dared to ask.

"Get off," Easalle ordered.

"What? But, why?" Burn stammered.

Would the beast eat us now? Had we angered him?

"Just get down." Easalle lowered his neck. "I am going to show you something."

One by one, we slid down. He raised his head and sat back on his haunches, exposing a large crystal among the scales on his broad chest

Easalle placed a forefoot gently across the gem, "This is where my heart once was. I gave up the space to save a . . ." he paused with a soft snort, ". . . dear friend. Only, it has become nothing more than a glittering, and weighty, coffin. And a voice in the back of my head." He shifted. "That is, until I find the lost island of magic, the only entrance to which is somewhere in these fool caves. I have been crawling down here for centuries and still have found no such opening."

"Why can't you fly to it?" I shrugged.

The dragon hung his head.

"Because the island doesn't exist." Burn shoved to the fore of the group. "Everybody knows that. If it did, the Trolls would have found it by now."

"For your information, Mister Know-it-all, the island does exist." Fire smoldered behind Easalle's fangs. "It is the way there that does not." He shook his great head. "Not yet anyway, but that is another matter, altogether. Right now, I need to get my harness back from those thieving Piskies, or I will never hear the end of it."

With Drake's help, we climbed back onto Easalle's back and continued trailing the Piskies to their hive.

Breaking through a clutch of bushes, we spotted a swarming mass. The Piskies' hive loomed, a wasp-like nest that matched Easalle in size. From a safe distance, we dismounted and watched. Multitudes of Piskie lights flitted through openings in the hive walls. Around and beneath the nest lay piles of treasures and trinkets. A glowing ring of armed Piskies guarded hive and hoard.

"Do you see the harness?" Easalle hissed from a cluster of bushes on the opposite side of the path. His red eyes shifted in the shadow of the leaves.

Hidden by branches, we crept along the edge of the path. I scanned the stacks of odd chains, baubles and glittering bits that made up the Piskies' hoard.

"What does a dragon harness look like anyway?" I whispered to the others.

Pillage shrugged before scurrying back to ask.

We held our positions with as much patience as we could muster. A rustle of leaves and a stifled giggle marked Pillage's return.

"Well?" Burn hushed her even as he asked. "What are we looking for, and what's so funny?"

Pillage could barely speak. She collapsed into a fit of stifled snickers. Our combined hiss shushed her as we surrounded her wiggling form.

"It's . . ." she squeaked.

I looked across the path toward the shaking head of the dragon, who rubbed a talon down the scaly ridge between his eyes.

"Pink!" The word exploded from her lips.

Burn clapped a hand over Pillage's mouth. "What's pink?" He demanded in a low voice.

"My harness." Easalle's talon's dragged across the sand. "The harness is made of pink and silver ribbon." Smoke curled from his lips and nostrils. "I know it's not very dragon-like. It was a gift."

Figuring it best not to laugh in the face of a dragon, no matter how embarrassing his situation, I stifled a giggle of my own. Burn and Plunder stared, scowls confirming their solidarity with Easalle's plight.

With new insight as to what to look for, we quickly spotted the item. The new problem was how to get it. It hung, draped, garland style, up and around the sides of the hive. The Piskies thought the harness a lovely decorative touch to the outer walls of their home. The idea of simply sneaking in and slipping out unnoticed seemed impossible. We needed a way to draw the Piskies' attention from the hive while someone retrieved the harness. We fell back to Easalle's position to inform him of the situation and devise a plan.

A short time later, Burn and I shimmied along the tangle of vines that snaked and twisted above the hive. Shifting webs of greenery made it no easy task. Part of me wished the twins were here in our place. At least they were a bit lighter. We closed on the hive. Shouts, clanging, and the crude lyrics of Piskie songs, hummed from the slits in the walls.

Through gaps in the leaves, I watched Pillage and Plunder stride along the path.

"Wow!" Plunder shook Burn's mask over his head. "It sure is lucky those mean little Piskies didn't get your mask," he called out over the din of the bawdy tunes, tempting the greedy little pirates.

"Yes!" Pillage shouted her reply. "It most certainly is!"

It was odd to hear the two speak complete sentences on their own.

The ring of guards swooped toward the twins. The hive shivered beneath us, the movement of hundreds of Piskie wings preparing to take flight. In a glowing explosion, a stream of Piskies flowed from a large hole in the side of the hive. Burn and I inched toward the center of our shared web of vines.

With a loud crack, branches shifted. We slid forward, smacking heads. And everything went terribly wrong.

The vines, not strong enough to hold our combined armored weight, snapped. One by one the strands of our viny web popped. We froze staring at one another with gritted teeth, in the moment before the last vines slithered away in all directions. We tried to push against one another and the empty air. We fell.

Under the weight of our flailing bodies, the hive crunched and tore like a ball of papier-mâché. Burn rubbed at newly raised bruises through his dented soup cans. I rolled onto my back atop the mound of broken hive.

"Oh dear." I grimaced at the angry speckled space above. "That's not good."

"Once again . . ." Burn scowled and gripped my wrist, ". . . you voice the obvious."

We leaped to our feet and sprinted for the path. I only managed a couple steps though before I remembered our errand. I made an about face. I dove into the pulpy scattering of hive remnants. Sifting through the debris, I retrieved the tangled pink ribbon and slung it over my head and shoulders. I caught up to Burn, and he reached over and hauled me onto the path. Easalle's harness fluttered and skipped behind me as we darted for the others.

"Run!" Burn and I snatched our masks from the twins, pulling them over our faces.

I looped the harness off my shoulders and over

Easalle's snout without pause.

The entire buzzing hive of angry, armed Piskies bared down the path. In a flash our companions turned and fled.

Drake tore down the path, passing Burn in a few long strides. Pillage and Plunder were upon us faster than I thought their little legs could move.

Easalle lumbered to take the rear, then swirled to a halt. "What am I thinking?"

We skidded in the sand and slid our attention a full one-eighty.

With a sweep of his tail, Easalle cleared a line in the foliage at the edge of the path. We ducked and lay out against the sand as his tail whipped just clear of our heads.

Easalle reared and belched the biggest fireball yet.

His flaming missile struck the pulsing wall of Piskies, bowling a perfect hole through the center. The remaining Piskies watched a fiery shower of their comrades rain down. One look at Easalle's glaring eyes and glowing row of fangs and they decided they had better things to do. Piskie wings hissed against leaves and petals as they fled into the darkness of the Jungle.

Easalle rippled a shiver from head to tail before turning with a noble air. He slipped the harness into place around his neck with a twist and gentle tug of his curved talons. "It's nice to know I still have it after all these years."

Awe held us in place.

Easalle cleared his throat in a wisp of smoke. "Thank you for your help, children. The little voice suggests collecting new weaponry and supplies from the Piskie hoard." He turned away.

"Easalle, wait." Still shaken from my shock, I sidled along the edge of the path to stand beside the dragon.

He sighed as I came around to face him. "I said, thank you." His grumble was gruff, but not wholly unkind.

"Yes," I said, gesturing to the others, "but we didn't."

Burn nodded. Drake made an awkward salute. The twins bounced and waved their little arms.

I tipped back on my heels to look up at Easalle. "If I wasn't a Troll, I think I'd like very much to be a dragon."

The great beast rolled his crimson eyes and lowered his head.

I threw my arms around his scaly neck as far as they would stretch. Pillage and Plunder ran up to join me. They flung themselves around his neck and showered his scales with kisses.

"Ugh. All right, all right. I get it." Easalle shook us off, but he could not hide his smile.

The jewel on Easalle's chest shimmered. For a moment, I could see the face of a young girl smiling back at me. When I looked again, it was only my reflection.

I stepped away. "Easalle, I hope someday you find the gateway you are looking for."

"Yeah." Burn added with a nod. "And after we rescue the Queen, we could even try to help you."

Easalle nodded once before lumbering into the darkness of the Jungle. There was no reason for a dragon to keep to the path. We watched until the tip of his tail disappeared through the dense leaves.

"Come on, then." Drake cleared his throat and I thought I caught him wipe the corner of his eye. "Let's see what those Piskies left behind."

Easalle was right, the Piskies had left a trove of weapons. We set to work pulling potential weaponry from the jumble of crushed hive and disheveled hoard. The Piskies were busy and far-reaching little creatures. From the chaotic mess, we sifted more than toys stolen from Trolls.

Burn discovered a large sword. His eyes glittered as he reached for it.

Drake lifted the weapon away. "I think that might be a bit too big for you."

He performed a few parries and thrusts.

Pillage and Plunder stumbled up behind Drake, brandishing a reflective piece of armor. They grinned when Drake caught sight of their find. He dropped the sword. I caught the gleam in Burn's eye and barred his path from the weapon.

"Fine." He kicked at the ground and marched over to see the armor.

Drake shook off his rusted suit as fast as the twins dug out new pieces to replace it. Burn and I smiled at each other, and dove into a nearby pile. Tossing and digging, we revealed more shining curves of plate and steel.

When the full gleaming suit hung on Drake's gangly frame, we stepped back a moment.

"How's the fit?" Drake twisted and pivoted. Poor timing to be asking really, he had shed his old armor and lost it randomly in the mounds surrounding us.

Burn sighed and pulled up the knight's gloves. Drake stood with arms and legs held slightly apart as Burn adjusted each piece.

I was impressed by the easy precision with which Burn fit each joint together. He made sure every strap and buckle was tightened properly. Each knot had to be pulled just right, Burn explained as he worked, so as not to cut off circulation or allow the metal pieces to slide along the chainmail.

It's extremely important to have everything just right so as not to cause chafing." He tugged on a strap and adjusted a final buckle.

"And he is very good at it." Drake straightened. "I have never experienced a rash or blister when Burn has assisted me with my armor. He is the finest squire a knight could hope for."

Burn blushed at the compliment, but made another adjustment without a word. Finally, after fitting a decorative shield to Drake's shoulder—the twins had to play human step stools for him to reach—Burn presented Drake with his new helmet.

Drake placed it upon his head.

I plucked a feather from my mask and handed it up to Burn. Drake bowed his head. Burn slipped the feather into the narrow funnel at the top of the helmet and stepped away.

Drake stood, marched in a small circle and flexed the joints. "Well done as usual, my good squire." He looked like a real knight and the suit fit as if made for him.

We gave a collective nod of approval.

"Come on." Burn snapped us out of our daze. "Let's load up and be off. Our knight in shining armor has a damsel to rescue."

Pillage and Plunder affixed a set of bicycle tires to a makeshift cart. It was no wagon tank but it would do. Burn and I loaded in the best of the weapons. We had no idea what we were going to be up against. The witch's castle could be crawling with minions as awful as the Dot, or guarded by Piskies, she might even have a dragon of her own.

The twins affixed four vines to our new transport and we each took hold of one as we set off. Drake strode ahead, knees high and chin up. Our new arsenal — a handful of wooden swords and a dozen pop guns with ammunition, a pair of buckler shields and two trash can lids — was far lighter than the previous. I hoped it would be enough.

We trudged onward, no one daring to ask, 'are we there yet?'

The way opened and brightened before us. The claustrophobic hold of the Jungle fell away. The light here had the same rippled effect as the hole at the top of the grotto. The ceiling of the cavern, at least a mile above, was a sky of crumpled glass. Overhead, water, moved and bubbled.

I shuddered, imagining the fate of anyone unfortunate enough to be beneath the liquid sky if it ever cracked.

"There." Drake leveled his shiny new sword to point into the distance.

I tore my eyes from the swimming ceiling to stare at the terror ahead. Turrets twisted up and out from the hard angles of the castle. Sharp spires sneered frighteningly close to the fragile sky.

For a moment, we cowered in the exposed emptiness of the castle grounds. We resumed our pace with half wanting to stop but knowing we needed to press on. Our footfalls sang against the cold, hard rocks. Each step echoed to the ceiling, ringing through the dread silence.

CHAPTER TEN:
SPIDERS, WITCHES, AND SAVING THE QUEEN

The castle loomed silent as we approached the jagged grin of the stone steps. We dropped our vines. The cart rattled to a stop. We stared. Fear of the evil that lay beyond the massive grey doors, held us rooted. My eyes ran the crazed scrollwork and twists of the carving, fighting to make sense of it.

No guards. No armies. Nothing we expected to find. Silent stone walls were the only sentries. With shaking hands, we strapped the essentials of weaponry to our armor.

Then, we clanked up the steps and aimed our popguns. Drake leaned into the door, but it failed to budge. We added our efforts. All five strained against the massive barrier. We heaved our shoulders, our feet scraping on the coarse stone steps. Slowly, a crack opened wide enough for us to squeeze through one by one between the double doors.

Armor clanked and pearls rattled as we stepped

into the inner court and stopped short.

This was not at all what I expected.

A tiny cottage nestled in the center of a lush lawn. An English style garden rambled into the vast expanse of green. Trails and tendrils of lush vines swirled and twisted along cobbled paths and up vibrant-leaved trees. Flowers in pastel and jewel tones speckled the lawn with bursts of color and beckoned bees and butterflies to dance through the air.

"I don't get it." Drake flipped back his visor and scratched at his forehead.

"We're . . ." The twins clung to Drake's legs.

"Scared." They finished in a whisper.

Burn appeared in my peripheral vision. "Creepy." His eyes fixed on the blooming pink rose bushes beneath the cottage's window frames.

"Are you sure this is the place?" I waved away a curious blue-winged butterfly that fluttered at my mask.

Burn shrugged and took a bold step toward the cottage. "Only one way to find out."

As if on cue, the door opened and a young woman backed out into the walkway. Her clothing was well worn, but not tattered, her apron, a stark white against the dense brown of her ankle-length dress. Long red braids looped back upon themselves and tucked neatly beneath a crisp white kerchief. She pulled something along the ground in front of her, but she hunched over it, blocking our view.

Burn raised his sword. The woman turned, revealing a bucket, the roped handle in her soft pale hands.

"No! It's poison or something!" Burn brandished

his sword and lunged.

I winced as the bucket rose up and the sword came down. With a splash that splattered clear across the cobbles, the contents of the bucket drenched Burn.

I pulled a soggy dust bunny from his mask. "If I were to guess, I'd say this poison is made of dishwater."

"Oh, dear me!" The woman let the bucket clatter to the stones. "You poor child. I didn't even see you."

With concern of danger laid aside for the moment, Drake and the twins snickered at Burn.

"Oh, don't worry. Burn needed a bath today any—" Drake gasped in recognition of the woman's bright clear eyes, youthful glowing features and red hair. He fell to one knee. "My Queen."

The twins clutched and wrinkled the starched apron. The Queen smiled, but there was a vacancy of confusion in her eyes. "I am sorry sir knight, children, I am no queen." She drew away from the embrace of the twins. "I am merely the servant and caretaker to the woman of this house." She returned her attention to the dripping Burn. "But please, come in and dry your . . ." she sought for the words, ". . . play clothes."

Gently, she took Burn by the hand and led him into the small home. Pillage and Plunder looked to Drake. His shoulders sagged. I helped him to his feet and followed after Burn and the Queen.

Drake removed his helmet and tucked it under his arm. He ducked low under the doorframe so as not to knock his head.

The cottage contained a cozy array of furnishings. On the wall furthest from the entryway stood a hearth. Beside it, Burn sat upon a stool, while the Queen helped him remove his armor and dried his face. She tousled his hair with a plush towel. I walked my gaze around the cobbled mantel and across the room to a round table with several stools cramped around it. A high-backed chair on one side of the table dwarfed the other pieces in the room.

"Please, the rest of you, sit." The Queen gestured to the table. "Make yourselves comfortable."

For no definable reason, we all avoided the chair seating ourselves upon the stools.

"Yes, do sit down." A scratchy voice coughed. A crumpled, old woman appeared from behind a gingham curtain opposite the table.

Her white hair hung to the floor, dragging like a veil as she pulled herself along with gnarled cane. Her steps were slow, but I sensed an unsprung energy in her movements.

"Oh, grandmother, I hope we did not wake you." The Queen hurried to help the old woman.

"No, no, no. Not at all my dear," the woman croaked back. "Tell me who our guests are." She eyed each of us in turn.

Her gaze sent shivers through me. Her eyes were black from pupil to iris. The twins gripped each other as the gaze stopped on them. Drake locked his knees and stood at attention. He stared straight ahead as if to avoid her scrutiny. She bent her crooked back and raised her head as far as she could, but still could not make eye contact. When she at last shuffled past and settled upon the high-backed chair, she focused her stare on Burn. If his waterlogged shirt and trousers had not given him

Goosebumps, the old woman certainly did.

"Kalleena," the old woman snapped. "When you are finished drying off that boy, offer our guests some refreshment." She smiled, but my skin crawled. "Cocoa perhaps, or tea for the gentleman knight."

The Queen wrapped Burn in the towel. "Yes, grandmother." She disappeared behind the curtain.

An uncomfortable silence fell over the room as the gingham fluttered into place. Drake cleared his throat. The legs of my stool squeaked against the floor. Burn sneezed.

The Queen reappeared, carrying a roll of clothing. "It may be a bit big." She shook the folds from the shirt. "It will have to do though until your clothes are dried." She handed the shirt to Burn and escorted him to the edge of the curtain.

He looked to us for reassurance. We glanced from the old lady to Burn as he disappeared behind the fold.

"Now, just hang those wet things over the tub," the Queen called through the fabric.

"Kalleena," the old woman crackled, "I think it would be best if those playthings be set outside instead of in our cozy living quarters." She turned her unnerving eyes upon Pillage, Plunder, Drake and I. "You four, as well. Scurry on outside and leave your dress-up clothes and toys beside the side of the door."

Drake and I exchanged a glance, then looked to the twins.

"Come, come, now." The old woman shooed us with her cane, the curved end of it stretched out to my nose. "Do not dawdle."

I felt a rush of familiar discomfort. Standing, I led the others back outside. The Queen followed and set Burn's armor beside the rose bushes whose thorns seemed larger than before.

"There now." She stacked the pile neatly and dusted her hands on her apron. "I'll put the water on. Hurry back inside."

The door closed behind her.

"Kalleena?" I pulled my mask from my face. "I have only seen the Queen once but are you sure that is her?" I brushed my frizzing curls from my face.

"She certainly looks like the Queen." Drake craned his neck and peered through the window.

Pillage and Plunder reached up to assist Drake with his armor. "She doesn't . . ."

They whimpered. "Know who . . ."

"We are." They removed their masks and stewpot helmets, setting them against the rose bushes.

"Yes." Drake's brow knit as he nodded. "The Queen knows and remembers all of her children." He crossed his arms. "So it cannot be her. Besides, the Queen is a prisoner of Arakne, and I saw no prisoners or witches in the cottage."

"But this is the witch's castle, isn't it?" I slid the last of my armor onto the ground. "Have you ever seen the witch?"

Drake, down to his chainmail, lifted the twins to shake them free of the last of their armor. "Maybe, the witch moved. We will replenish our strength and ask Kalleena and her grandmother." He didn't hide his shudder. "There is no use wandering in circles if they can tell us where to find Arakne."

I fluffed my dress. "Fine."

Drake ducked back into the cottage, Pillage, Plunder and I parading behind.

Burn was seated as far from the old woman as possible, his arms crossed defiantly over his chest. I could not help but snicker at his attire. The nightshirt Kalleena had given him was far too large, and patterned with dainty flowers, certainly not the most dignified ware for a knightly squire. He glared and roughly tugged one frilly shoulder into place.

I settled one seat away from Burn, placing Pillage between us. Plunder flopped onto the stool on the other side of me, leaving a stool between him and the old woman. Drake folded into the seat on the other side of Burn, his knees practically to his chin.

"Oh, I do hope you are comfortable." Kalleena looked specifically at Drake.

We assured her we were quite comfortable, though we all felt the dreadful unease of the old woman's presence. Her eyes and cane loomed in our thoughts.

Kalleena set to work with table settings and hot water.

"How long have you two lovely ladies lived so far out here?" Drake took a warm cookie from the plate at the center of the table.

"Years." The old woman turned her glare on Drake.

"Oh." Drake swallowed. Seated he could do nothing to avoid her eyes. He snapped up another cookie and focused on chewing.

Pillage and Plunder scooted their stools closer to mine.

Kalleena returned with a delicate china set. She

placed a cup and saucer in front of each of us. The teakettle whistled over the heat of the fire. She wrapped a towel around the curve of the handle and lifted the kettle to a trivet on the table. The whistle subsided and we shifted in silence again. From the cupboards she took another tray on which sat a neat stack of dark chocolate squares balanced beside a delicate bowl of sugar cubes, a set of silver tongs and a pitcher of cream as white as Kalleena's apron.

She placed the tray beside the steaming kettle and the plate of cookies.

Dropping a square of chocolate into the old woman's china cup, she followed it with a pair of sugar cubes and a drizzle of cream. Lastly, setting a silver spoon into the cup, she leaned across the table and lifted the steaming kettle. A narrow stream of water arced into the cup and over the contents within. Dark liquid rose into view. Kalleena set the kettle in the center of the table and danced the spoon around the inside of the cup, careful not to click the china.

I watched in awe. I had never seen hot cocoa made in such a way. When she finished stirring, Kalleena sat on her stool beside the old woman.

"Now, remember," she said, putting a silver spoon into Plunder's cup, which held an extra sugar cube, "always rest the spoon against the edge of the cup. It prevents the china from cracking from the heat." She filled Plunder's cup with the hot water.

We could not take our eyes off her. She had to be the Queen. I sensed it to my core. Why did she not know us? But, if she was the Queen, where was the witch, Arakne, who had taken her captive? I leaned away to allow Kalleena to pour the water, and something slipped from my apron pocket.

It clattered and bounced as it struck the stone floor.

The others leaned to see. In her distraction, Kalleena overflowed the teacup. Hot cocoa dribbled onto the white linen of the table covering. "Oh dear!" She disappeared behind the curtain. "That will stain if I don't sop it up quickly."

When I retrieved the rattle from against the table leg. The bell came loose from the handle. Kalleena returned, carrying a towel and small brick of soap and saw me holding the two pieces.

"Oh, Tierannie, your rattle." She set down the soap and towel. "I am sure we can fix it."

She took the toy from my hands and fit the pieces together. The light had returned to the Queen's eyes.

Plunder knocked into me. He tugged at my apron. Burn, Pillage and Drake backed from the table, the look on their faces a combination of terror and confusion. My gaze strayed over the table to where the old woman sat.

"Now, dearies." The woman hunched forward, her hair falling over her face. " You know how Arakne hates toys." Her body lurched. "Children should be seen and not heard!"

The Queen's attention tore from the rattle.

Drake dove, throwing the Queen clear as the witch flew across the table, through the empty space and landed against the wall of the cottage.

"That was too close." Drake pulled himself off the floor and reached to help the Queen, drawing back with a start.

Her clothes lay crumpled and empty beneath him.

Drake and I bashed heads as we dug through the pile. "Where did she go?"

"I would be more worried about where Arakne intends to go!" Burn's comment pulled our attention to the witch.

Where the old woman's hump had been, eight hairy legs had sprouted. Her face and long white hair remained, but her body had assumed the shape of a giant spider.

"I want to wake up now." I pinched my arm. "This is a dream. I fell into the river, was knocked unconscious and—"

Drake grabbed Pillage and Plunder, one under each arm, and dove for the cupboards. Burn slid with me under the curtain. The old woman-turned-spider, landed in the space we had occupied only a moment before. She smashed the wooden table with a slam of one tremendous leg. A spray of cocoa, water, and cookie crumbs fountained in every direction.

"I thought you said she didn't use magic!" I shook Burn by the shoulders.

The witch's legs crashed in succession as we crawled along the wall toward the front door.

"She doesn't!" Burn shouted over the hissing chatter of the spider.

"Well, then, what is your smarty-pants explanation for how she did that?" I shoved him clear as another spider leg lashed out.

Arakne blocked the doorway. Drake held a rolling pin like a sword. Pillage and Plunder cowered behind his legs.

"Drake!" Burn swung a broken stool. "Run!" He lobbed the chair at the witch's back.

She turned on us.

Drake grabbed the twins and bolted for the door. Between the witch's legs, Burn and I watched them disappear.

The witch almost upon us, our backs against the wall, weaponless and alone, Burn and I wrapped our arms around one another and sank into the corner.

"You know I never really thought you were stupid." Burn closed his eyes.

"Yeah, well, I was in awe of your knowledge of this place." I squeezed my eyelids shut.

We squished down as small as possible. The witch's rank and rasping breath filled my senses.

Suddenly, my ears rang with the sound of shattering glass.

Drake, clad in chainmail and helmet, crashed through the window. He landed between the witch and us. "All right, witch!" He held his fists up. "Let's see what you've got!"

"Drake!" Burn pushed away and to his feet. "Where's your sword?"

Drake looked at his empty hands. He smiled weakly at the giant spider. The witch's wrinkled face split to reveal a double row of jagged yellowed fangs.

"Run." Drake choked back the crack in his voice.

He scooped Burn and I from the floor and tossed us out the broken window. We rolled into the yard and stopped short of Pillage and Plunder, where they piled armor onto one another. Burn and I leaped to our feet and did the same. Drake's body flew out the window. I lunged forward, saving my mask from breaking his fall.

Burn and I each took an arm to help the knight to his feet.

"Keep moving!" Drake gathered armor into his lanky arms.

We secured masks and helmets, grabbed weapons, and prepared to run, when the house exploded behind making us hit the dirt. I looked back though I really didn't want to.

Arakne, having blown through the thatched roof, landed with an earth trembling shudder on the ground behind us.

We did not wait for her to leap again.

Gathering our fallen weapons we darted across the lawn. Pillage and Plunder slid and rolled under a row of thickly thorned rose bushes. Drake's long legs carried him far across the barren field. We lost the spider, and in the process, one another, in the twisted wilds of the shifting garden.

My mind reeled as I collapsed, heaving, into a brush-covered ravine. My eyes darted about in search of some sign of the others. Splitting up might confuse the witch, but it didn't offer us the security of numbers.

"Tierannie." A voice hissed above the bushes. "Tierannie?"

I did not trust the rustling above me and met it with my blade. Burn's face appeared at the point.

"Put that away." He pushed the weapon aside. "It's only me." He glanced over his shoulder. "Get down." He tumbled through the leaves and settled in the dirt beside me.

"Where are the others" I tipped my head to the surface.

He lifted his mask from his face. "I don't know."

He rubbed at his nose. "Do you know where Arakne is?"

I shook my head.

"I hope she hasn't found the twins." He threw his head into his hands. "Agh!"

I shushed him with a finger to his lips.

"Pillage and Plunder are my responsibility. How could I have lost them?" His voice was rising again. "At the worst possible time! I have failed them!"

"Shhh!" It was a harsh sound, but I had no desire for the witch to find us.

I took Burn by the shoulders and turned him to face me. Tears dripped from the corners of his eyes. I caught a breath of shock. I hadn't thought Burn could cry.

"Listen." For a moment, I was at a loss, before the words tumbled out. "Burn, Up There kids our age are not even allowed to babysit, no less have sole responsibility for younger children. You've done a good job with Pillage and Plunder. They know how to defend themselves." I allowed a small smile to my lips. "More importantly, they know how to hide."

He bowed his head.

I shook his shoulders to make him look at me. "You have not failed them. We'll find them, and together we will stop that witch, the same way we stopped her ugly Dot and those horrible Piskies. Together."

"The dragon actually stopped the Piskies." He sniffled.

"Whatever." I rolled my eyes. "We can do this. We just have to regroup."

He nodded and wiped at his face. My speech seemed to have worked. I honestly had no idea what

I was talking about, but Burn was Burn again. That was all that mattered.

We crawled along the shallow well of the trench, calling steadily but quietly for the others. Suddenly, the witch's spidery legs thumped along the ground above us. She paused. We held our breath until the scurry of legs faded into the distance. As we came around another wall of bushes, we ran out of ditch to hide in. We had arrived back behind the cottage.

Movement shadowed through the rear window. I pointed it out to Burn. He nodded. With a last look around to make sure the field was clear, we ran, hunched low, and ducked under the window frame.

Pulling up to peer through the glass, side by side our heads turned to scan the scene. I froze.

Everything was neat and clean, as if a giant spider-witch had never smashed the table and stools.

I pointed to the roof and mouthed the words, "No hole."

Burn and I exchanged baffled looks.

Kalleena—the Queen—strolled about the house, a dust rag in hand, singing softly. Though we could not make out the whole tune, it sounded familiar.

"Double creepy." Burn shook his head.

I grabbed the collar of his shirt and drew him to the ground. I put my fingers to my mask's lips and gave him a frustrated glare. He shot the look right back at me and threw up his hands. I brought my attention to the window. Burn crawled up beside me. We watched in silence and confusion as Kalleena cleaned. She approached the table and paused, the notes of the song caught in her throat. Staring down, she bent. When she stood she held the broken rattle, handle in one hand, bell in the other. My name formed on her lips, though whether she said it out loud or not, I could not tell.

"It is rude to peek in windows, children." The witch snarled behind us.

We spun. She had returned to her old woman shape, belief was fleeting, when we saw what she held in each hand.

The twins squirmed and kicked in Arakne's gnarled grasp. Their mouths were sealed with a mesh of webbing.

"Let them go!" Burn advanced on the old woman.

"Ah, ah." She gave Burn a wicked glare. "You are going to be good little children, unless you want me to make your pretty Queen disappear again."

Burn retreated with an apologetic gaze to Pillage and Plunder. The twin's shoulders slumped as they stopped struggling against the witch's grip.

"That's a good boy." The witch purred. "Now, why don't we all go inside and have a little chat. Maybe some more hot cocoa."

Burn and I followed Arakne's veil of white hair to the front of the cottage. She opened the door and filed us through.

"We have guests, Kalleena." The witch announced.

The Queen tucked the broken rattle into her apron.

"I'll set the table, grandmother." Kalleena scurried into the kitchen.

With a sharp look, the witch bid us to be seated. Kalleena moved about the kitchen, exactly as before. She gathered cups, a tray, and arranged them on the table. She pumped water from the sink into a kettle.

I leaned over the table toward the witch. "What did you do with Drake you old hag?"

She glared.

Pillage and Plunder, still gagged, pulled me to my seat. Burn stared straight ahead.

"Drake?" The witch tapped a bony finger against her sharp chin. "Oh, right, the cowardly knight you arrived with. I am afraid I did nothing with him." She clawed her crooked fingers at the air. "He ran off and left you poor children to fend for yourselves."

"That's a lie!" Burn slammed his hands on the table.

Kalleena paused in her mechanical movements.

"Young man, what do you mean raising your voice to grandmother?" She stared, wide-eyed at Burn. "If you cannot behave yourself, I am going to have to ask you to leave."

Burn balled his fists, but drew his hands to his lap.

The witch's smile was jagged. Kalleena, returning to her duties, she hung the kettle over the fire. As she carried out each task, she seemed completely unaware the she had done all of this not an hour or less before.

"Kalleena," I said, beckoning her to my side, "will we be having some of those wonderful cookies you served us before?"

"Pardon?" She looked bewildered.

"Cookies," the witch snarled. "Kalleena, our guests would like some cookies. Now, don't dawdle."

Kalleena nodded apologetically and scurried to fetch the cookies from the same cupboard as before.

The witch shifted her awful eyes upon me. "You

foolish, foolish child. She doesn't remember a thing before we walked in here. It would serve you well not to try to give her any more reminders."

I leaned back from the table, but kept my gaze on the old woman.

Burn got to the question before me. "Why does she not remember? You have no magic to make her forget."

"Oh, but I do." The witch folded her long fingers together. "My magic is that I know what Kalleena used to be. What she was before she was allowed to remember what magic was." She leaned into her arched fingers. "The longer she forgets, the more magic I can collect from her. I am draining it from her. Your Queen has no power to replenish her magic when she is away from the throne room and her silly little moon lake. Removed from her sanctuary, she is easy prey."

"Her magic is no magic." I whispered the words Burn had told me so far back in our journey. "Of course." I stood.

Confused and shocked looks scurried around the table.

"It is like Mother taught in science lesson." Even Arakne seemed befuddled by my words. I had no intention of dumbing things down, though. I might be able to use this moment to my advantage.

I rolled my shoulders, straightened up, and cleared my throat. I circled to the back of the stool and began to march around the table. "When a lot of energy is packed into a small space," I said, as my hands clenched together, "if another, more open space is offered, the energy flows to it eagerly." I opened out my hands.

I had no real idea what I was talking about, but the witch did not know that. She glared with her wicked, black-pooled eyes, angry, but interested. I had to get her guard down.

From the corner of my eye, I could see Kalleena also burning to make sense of my words. They had never heard of science down here. Science and logic were a commodity of the Up There, a place they all saw as fantasy to their fantastic reality.

"Of course, once the new vessel is completely full, it cannot take on any more energy." I seated myself near the witch's chair. "That is unless it wishes to burst." I bugged my eyes out wide and spread my fingers, palms to the witch.

She jumped back. Kalleena edged closer to the table, absorbed by my lesson. They all were.

"So," I fed more information, "no matter how much the new vessel takes on, there may well be more energy still bumping about in the original one."

I pulled the river rock from my pocket and slammed it onto the table.

"In other words . . . " We all shifted our attention when Kalleena spoke. ". . . there is still some magic in me yet."

Her fingertips sizzled with a pale glow. A spark leapt between her outstretched digits. Slowly, shakily, she raised her hands, arms outstretched. Higher, higher, level with her shoulders, above, and up. Above her head, a small green glow appeared between her palms.

The glow sparked and grew, brighter and more intense, until we were forced to close our eyes. Then, like someone had pulled the plug, the light went out.

My eyes flew open.

The Queen stood, hands still above her head, nothing between her hands.

She looked up. She swayed.

A crash at the other side of the cottage gripped our attention. The door flew off its hinges. Fully armored and armed, Drake burst into view. With a crash, the roof was torn off the cottage. Easalle's dark-scaled snout loomed through the opening. We released a collective sigh of relief as Drake dove to the aide of the fainting Queen. She slid into his waiting arms.

The witch cackled.

"Drake?" The Queen's eyes fluttered as she gazed up at her champion.

Even in the shadow of his helmet, I could see the blush tint Drake's cheeks.

"How very sweet," the witch growled.

She began her transformation into her spider form. Drake set the Queen upon a stool, out of harm's way. He stood between the Queen and the witch, his sword brandished in defense.

"The cowardly knight, or should I say runty giant, returns to rescue the Troll Queen." Her spider legs shot out from the seams of her black dress. Her head twisted on her neck to look at Easalle, "And he brought with him a gallant steed."

A high-pitched drone pulsed the air. I covered my ears and sought the origin of the sound. A dark mass appeared above Easalle. His head bobbed once, then again, before he swept his great neck around.

The witch sneered as hundreds of Piskies darted

around Easalle's head and neck, jabbing at him with their pointy weapons. Fighting to knock them away, he lumbered from the cottage and out of sight.

I could hear his roar, and the crash of his tail as he battled the throngs of tiny pirates.

"It is good to have so many friends willing to come when called." The witch's body melted with an ugly lurch into shape of the spider.

She loomed even larger than before. She lowered her head and hissed in my face, her fang sticky with venom, and her breath a toxic reek.

"It seems your fantastic theory from the Up There has never been tried on magic!" She screeched.

I backed away but had nowhere to run. The giant witch-faced-spider had cornered me. The boiling kettle whistled on the hearth. The witch shifted her attention to the sound. I dove between the hairy spider legs. With bare hands, I tore the iron kettle off its hook. Scalding water sloshed over the monster's back.

Arakne screamed. Hissing, clicking, and wailing as I imagined a ten foot spider might. I too wailed. The iron handle seared into my palms. The kettle clattered to the ground. Twin blisters bloomed across my palms.

"Why. You. Naughty. Little. Girl!" The witch screamed. "You naughty, wicked, little beast!" She jabbed the air with her vicious spider legs.

"Look who's talking!" I screamed back at her.

The pain in my hands throbbed and pumped tears from my eyes. Two pair of hands took hold of wrists and hauled me out of the spider's range.

Pillage, Plunder and I tumbled clear of crashing debris and struck the pillared mantle, crashing into Burn. Regaining our footing, we bolted away.

The four of us collided into a looming giant. This one was on our side. We gaped in awe of the very noble looking Drake. In one great step he passed over us and leveled his sword at the witch. The spider shifted and reared back on her hind legs, mandibles clacking like hammers.

The knight held his ground. With a battle cry only a giant could know, he lunged at the beast and plunged his blade, hilt deep, into the spider's bulbous body.

A stomach churning squish resounded. He recoiled from the strike. Green-black ooze glubbed from the wound.

Arakne wailed louder than when I had poured the water upon her back.

For a moment, Drake lost his nobility. He turned pale, then green. Easalle appeared above, peering through the open roof. "Nasty annoying Piskies!" His wings fanned a rush of putrid wind from the wounded spider.

Arakne's blood blackened and matted her hair. Her legs struggled to stay beneath her bulbous body. But even as she slipped in the pooling ooze, the slash in her gut knitted, and the burned flesh bubbled back into shape.

Drake dripped with the sticky monster fluids and looked green. Despite the sickening scene, we cheered.

A tap on my shoulder drew my attention. "Take it." The Queen held the broken rattle out to me in trembling hands.

She had grown weak from the witch draining her magic. I took the rattle from her, but dropped it as pain seared through my palms. Pillage and Plunder dove from behind and caught the Queen as she slipped to her knees. The last of her strength slipping away. Burn snatched the rattle off the floor.

The Queen leaned heavily on the twins. "Drake cannot stop her. Even a dragon is no match now." She closed her eyes and sighed. When she opened them again, the last of her power glistened in the pale pools. "Take the rattle, Tierannie!"

"I can't." I turned my palms to her.

She pulled one weak arm out of Pillage's grasp and tugged at her apron. It slid to the floor.

"Burn!" the Queen commanded in the most royal voice she could muster. "Wrap her wounds."

Burn nodded and did as he was told. He tore the apron in two. I winced and cried out as he wrapped the first strip of cloth around my hand.

"Be brave." His voice was stern, but his eyes were kind. He knotted the bandage across the back of my hand. I sniffed back another cry of pain as he bound the other hand and tied the knot.

"Quickly!" We followed the Queen's concerned gaze.

Anew cloud of Piskies swarmed their way into the cottage. They surrounded the witch, darting at Drake and Easalle, hampering their attacks. Easalle, fearing to set the thatched cottage aflame, snapped at zipping Piskies with his large jaws. Pillage and Plunder pulled the Queen to the far end of the room. Burn and I carried each half of the rattle. We cowered. The spider-witch struck a mighty blow. Drake's armored body careened into the front door. His dented form clanged in a heap onto the threshold.

"Drake!" Burn tossed aside the rattle and ran to his fallen hero.

At Drake's side, Burn picked up the fallen sword, which was as long as he was tall. Positioned between Drake and the advancing witch, he raised weapon. The heavy blade quivered in his hands.

"Drake is not a coward!" Burn screamed, tears streamed down his cheeks. "I knew he didn't leave us!"

"Actually, Burn," Drake murmured, pushing up from the floor and onto his hands and knees, "I am a coward, but I am more afraid of losing my family than of that monster."

Burn focused on the witch, ignoring Drake's words.

The witch's legs trembled with every step. Though the Piskies swirled around her in a fog of wings, still her injuries were clear. Her white hair hung in patches. One eye was gashed closed. No coward could do to this beast what Drake had.

I took a cautious step toward Burn and Drake. My toe nudged something. My eyes were drawn to the silver glinting in the light of the Piskies. The rattle. I winced in pain, gathering the two pieces into my bandaged hands. I didn't know what the Queen intended I do with a baby's toy against a monster, but I wanted with all my heart to believe in her magic. Pillage, Plunder, Burn and Drake certainly had unwavering faith.

The rattle burned in my palms. I dropped it once more. I stared at the thing. The bell slowly rotated. Of its own accord, it aligned with its other half. It leapt from my left hand to connect with the handle in my right. Warmth flooded down the handle and through my hands.

I shook it to be sure I had not imagined the transformation.

The magic had only just begun. The bell pulled upright and my hand moved with it. I jangled the toy, gently at first, then with more force. As if commanded by something deep in my core, I shook the rattle, more rapidly. The marble within sang against the inside of the bell.

From between the slits in the bell a glow emanated. I stared. I hoped whatever was happening was meant to help.

The witch halted her advance on Burn and Drake. The Piskie cloud around her seemed to shift in my direction. The light from the rattle reflected in her remaining black eye. Burn, Drake, even Easalle were captivated by the strange event taking place within the rattle. Pillage, Plunder and the Queen remained behind me, out of my line of sight, but I could feel their eyes upon the dancing, bell. Only the drone of Piskie wings and the wild jangling of the rattle filled the air.

I extended my arm. With a resounding ping, the glowing marble struck the first dent in its prison. I jumped, but held tight to the handle. Another dent and another jump on my part. Then another. The dents came slow at first. Ignoring the pain searing through my palms, I gripped the rattle firmly. Soon, the pings blended together in a rapid staccato of clangs resonating through the cottage until, at last, like the pctals on a flower, the bell of the rattle peeled back and released the marble.

I swung my free arm over my eyes to shield them from the impending impact from a wild marble. We threw ourselves on to the cottage floor. When nothing happened, I lowered my arm from my eyes. A long breath escaped my lips.

Freed from its prison, the marble hovered like a firefly. It had clearly worked out its tantrum against the walls of the rattle. Quietly, it now hovered and bobbed in the center of the open bell.

The Piskies, sensing they were on the losing side, abandoned the witch, an angry buzz that faded into the distance. Arakne wobbled on her spidery legs, seemingly smaller than before. Easalle's head peered through the opening in the roof. Leaning on Drake's sword, Burn rose from the floor. Drake tugged at the hem of Burn's nightshirt. He looked away from the marble long enough to assist the knight to his feet. From behind me, Pillage and Plunder guided the Queen.

All eyes were drawn away from the marble when the Queen rose to a regal stance.

"No," Arakne's fading voice hissed. "No." Conviction wavered in her tone.

She drew her legs beneath her, one by one. The wounds Drake inflicted had taken a toll. Her remaining eye grew wild as she watched the gently bobbing glow. "One of the seven keys?" She choked out a scream. "It was in a child's toy!"

The marble did not look like any key I had ever seen. Of course, not much about this world was like anything I had ever seen.

Arakne took a tumbling, trembling step toward me. She extended a twisted leg toward the rattle. I held my ground and the rattle through the wave of fear and pain. It was enough to activate yet another of the marble's tricks. A thin stream of pale green light shot from the orb and struck the witch directly in the middle of her pale forehead.

She wailed.

The witch writhed in the beam of light. Another beam struck out in the direction of the Queen. All eyes followed it.

"The keys know where magic belongs. "The Queen held out a hand to catch the light.

The witch screamed. Her body expanded and contracted in gruesome heaves. Her wailing shattered the windows into shards that exploded out over the garden. Teacups that had managed to survive the earlier battle trembled to pieces where they lay.

I covered one of my ears. The others did the same. Still clinging to the great sword, Burn suddenly shifted off his feet and pressed against me. Drake covered our outer ears with his elbows as he protected his own ears with his hands. Only the Queen seemed unaffected by the piercing sound.

The kerchief blew free of her hair. Her braids uncoiled. Like a waterfall breaking from winter's frozen hand, red hair cascaded free.

The witch, what remained of her, expanded in a final heave. With a pop that was audible even through our muffled senses, she exploded in blobs of slimy, sticky black ooze. Everything in the cottage dripped in vile goo. Save for the Queen, whose glowing form stood untouched within a protective orb.

Light retreated back to the marble as it clattered out of orbit. The petals of the rattle curled gracefully back into place. The head of the rattle tumbled from the handle. Still too stunned and sticky from the defeat of the witch, I failed to catch it. It skipped across the floor and stopped with a final ping against a shard of teacup.

A squish of ooze stretched between my ear and Burn's as he pulled his face away from mine.

"I'm sure I can fix it." He bent to pick up the rattle. "Not with magic, though."

I smiled. "So, is that it then?" I shook my fingers free of the sticky goop.

"That's . . ." Pillage chimed in.

"It!" Plunder led the Queen to us.

"That is the end for Arakne." A beautiful smile spread beneath the Queen's glimmering eyes. "The witch could no longer contain the magic she had stolen. The power of the key was too much. It destroyed her."

"It sure did." Still green, Drake flung a clump of spidery ooze from his gauntlet. "Ick."

Burn tapped against Drake's armored thigh and offered the hilt of the knight's weapon. The knight peered down at his squire and took the heavy sword. "I am not sure I will be needing this ever again." Drake looked over the blade.

"Keep it just the same." Easalle's voice boomed from above. "A noble knight deserves to carry a fine sword." He shrugged off the last of the Piskie bodies that clung to his great shoulders. "Just promise you won't go slaying dragons with it."

Drake saluted and blushed. He rubbed at the back of his head when he caught the Queen smiling at him.

He stared a moment at the points of his armored

toes, then fell to one knee.

The Queen lifted his face in her hands to look into his eyes. "Stand, good knight. Good friend."

Drake turned the same shade of red as the Queen's hair. He gazed into her eyes. With him on one knee, they were nearly eye-to-eye. She leaned toward him. Confusion widened his eyes. The Queen pressed her lips softly to those of her knight.

"Ewwww!" A chorus of voices called from all around us. Trolls peeked between crumbled walls and through shattered windows.

The Queen stepped back. Giggling faces peered on making mock kissing noises. Burn and Plunder made the most awful faces of disgust. I put my arm over Pillage's shoulder and we sighed.

The Queen held out a hand to Drake and bid him rise.

"Well," she addressed her Trolls, "now that we are all together again, the only thing left to do is head home to celebrate our brave heroes."

A resounding agreement banged on the walls and windowsills and roared in their cheers.

CHAPTER ELEVEN:
GOING HOME AND HOME AGAIN

Easalle's great form rambled from behind the ruins as we exited into the yard.

"Wait." I dared to take the Queen by the hand and lead her to the dragon's side. "Easalle."

The dragon swung his long neck to face us. "The Piskies are gone. The witch is gone. You have your Queen. Let this old dragon get on with his journey."

"But, Easalle . . ." I looked from the dragon to the Queen. ". . . maybe it is possible for us to help you now."

The Queen smiled. "You are the dragon who has wandered my caverns for some centuries."

"You know me?" Easalle's brow knit raising his horns.

The Queen tilted her head. "I know of you. A dragon is a hard thing to hide in so narrow a space."

Easalle huffed. He lowered his head to the Queen's level.

"You are seeking something?" The Queen laid a pale hand on the dark scales of the dragon's snout.

Easalle shifted on his feet. "A gateway." He looked to me as if I could help him explain. "I seek the Island of Windfall. My purpose is pure."

"I believe it is." The Queen noted the large crystal on Easalle's chest. "I can open the gateway."

This brought light to Easalle's eyes. "That your words confirm its existence is more than I have hoped for."

"But, you will still have to seek out the entrance on your own." The Queen frowned. "The doorway is something only those with a purpose can discover. But, the way will not be locked to you." The Queen offered with a gentle smile.

Easalle drew his head back. His lips curled back in a smile that exposed his fangs. We were not afraid, though some of the Trolls did shy away. Easalle was a kind soul, at least, to those he counted as allies.

"Thank you." Easalle bowed his head once more to the Queen of the Trolls. "You will understand if I hurry on my way. The Trolls may always count on this dragon in times of need though."

Drake marched to meet us. "May you find your quest easy. Though, if you need a knight, I am at your service." He bowed to the dragon.

We waved a farewell as, Easalle's silhouette lumbered into the distant edge of the Jungle.

The return trip moved smoothly, though not in haste. The entire tribe of Trolls filled the path, the Queen and Drake in their center, hand in hand. The jingling, clanking, stomping of children in masks and cans made a music that could certainly be heard for a great distance. Choruses of Troll songs shivered through jungle leaves with waves of cheers and squeals thrown about for good measure. I imagined it much like the sounds from an elementary school at the last bell on the final day of classes. The journey allowed time to ask so many questions I had not considered earlier. Most importantly, I wanted to be certain the witch was truly dead, and all her minions destroyed.

The Queen assured me Arakne was gone, but another witch might sooner or later take her place.

"There can be no peace between the powers of good and evil." She explained. "For without both there would be no balance and life would become stagnant. Without trials there can be no jubilation upon triumph over them. We learn about ourselves when we overcome the obstacles that block our way." She leaned her head upon Drake's shoulder. "We learn about friends and family as well."

Drake reddened for the zillionth time since the kiss at the cottage.

"What if we cannot rescue you the next time?" She smiled down at me and set a gentle hand upon my head.

"I have no fear of such things. When my time comes, it will come. Until then though, I trust that my Trolls and my knight, will protect me the best they can." She leaned into Drake. She closed her hand around the handle of the rattle as I carried it. "The keys know where the magic in this world belongs and where it will do the most good."

"The keys." I plunged into my next question. "Are they all hidden each one in a different toy on the shelves in the grotto? And how did it do that thing back in the cottage. And how did the rest of the Trolls know where to find us?"

The Queen's laugh bubbled at my barrage of questions. "Oh my! It would be very foolish indeed to hide something so powerful in the grotto. Why, as often as those toys are lost or broken, I would never be able to find any of them."

"Then why the rattle?" I held out the toy.

The Queen's loving smile shown down on me, "Until you came back to us, Tierannie, all Trolls swore never to move that rattle. Burn was most adamant about this."

I was not certain what to make of this information, so I moved on to my next question.

"Will the Jungle be as dangerous now that Arakne is dead?" I looked off the path into the dark leaves at either side. There might be something to safety in numbers, but there were so many things I had come across thus far I was not eager for any new surprises.

"Of course it will." The Queen laughed lovingly. "What would be the fun if everything in life were simple?"

"A little danger builds character." Burn pranced in front of me. "Why? Are you scared?" He tucked his hands into his armpits and flapped his bony elbows. "Tierannie's a chicken! Tierannie's a chicken! Bawk! Bawk! Ba-bawk!"

He ran ahead when I swung out to grab him. "Yeah! Now who's the chicken?"

Ahead, the vibrant reds and golds of his mask danced between the throng of Trolls. I was pretty sure Burn was off to tell 'his boys' that he had saved my foolish, stupid girl butt a hundred times over the course of the quest. Part of me wondered what fun it would be to tell the boys that Burn, their fearless leader, had cried like a baby when our adventure had reached some difficult moments. I would keep that little tidbit of information tucked away, but I would tell Pillage, if I left before I needed to use it.

"Wait for me, Burn!" Plunder scurried after his mentor.

"Sometimes they act like normal children." The Queen smiled out over the crowd. "Sometimes they are far stronger than their physical age."

Plunder's little legs pumped and his arms parted the crowd as the small boy fought to join his clan. I smiled at the thought that passed through my mind; Drake, Burn, Plunder, a short but noble line of knights. Pillage fell into step beside me. Though she was the one smiling up at me, I could not help but see myself as Pillage's humble student. Physically Pillage was, of course, younger, but she had been through far more in this world than I. Even in the wake of this adventure, Pillage was in many ways my senior. I had learned so many things from the small girl. Pillage and Plunder both had proven themselves as worthy allies.

As Pillage kept pace, I found myself considering new ways to avoid speaking about my lingering desire to leave. While I was not certain when or how I would go home, I knew I would have to do so, in the end.

Passing the still empty wreckage of the Piskie hive, I thought of Easalle, Pillage, Plunder, Drake, the Queen, the Muses, even Burn. I did not want to hurt any of my new family by leaving. In so short a time. As we walked, I thought of how falling into the Grotto the first time seemed to be a complete accident. The second attempt, while intentional, might well have been a complete coincidence.

Ahead of me, the Queen of the Trolls walked arm in arm with her knight. If I asked to be sent back, the Queen could do it, I had no doubt, but what of the chance of seeing any of them again? I had to be sure that the choice I made would be the right one.

Our steady course slowed to a halt, as if in answer to my need for more time. Before the parade of Trolls loomed the great ivory pillars of the Hall of Muses.

The halfway point to home. Had I thought that? I shook the thought from my head.

"Why have we stopped?" Pillage cupped her hands around her mouth and called out over the crowd.

Drake looked out over the mass of Trolls. ""Looks to me like no one wants to go up the stairs."

"Well, why not?" Pillage hopped up and down, trying to see over the sea of heads. "Are they too tired to climb?" Pillage and I pushed through the throng to the front.

Someone grabbed my shoulder as we brushed past. I turned to shrug the hand away.

"Why have we stopped?" Burn released my shoulder.

Plunder stood beside him, his expression puzzled.

"It seems no one wants to climb the steps to the Hall of Muses." I continued my push to the front of the pack.

A line of Trolls, with masks pushed back upon their heads, starred in awe up the massive stairs.

I peered over the shoulder of the nearest Troll, and looked for some cause for the delay.

"Have none of you ever seen the Hall before?" I asked.

One of Burn's boys spoke up. "No one has gone in there. Not in a very long time." The expression on his face was not one of awe and joy as I would have expected.

I had been so excited to revisit the home of the Muses and see the changes complete, I had not considered that anyone might not want to make the trip.

"Don't you want to see all the beautiful works of art?" I tugged at the boy's wrist.

"Yes!" Plunder's head bobbed into view.

"Beautiful!" Pillage took the hand of another girl in the line.

"But, what about the Dread Dot?" A girl down the line tipped back her bright pink mask, revealing pale blue eyes wide with fear.

"Yeah." The boy whose arm I continued to tug at shuddered. "What if it caught us in there?"

I looked to Pillage. She smiled at Burn, who rolled his eyes at Plunder. We burst into fits of laughter.

The boy glared. "What are you laughing at?"

You are . . . afraid . . . of . . ." Burn fell over laughing before he could finish his sentence.

"The . . ." Pillage fell into giggles.

"Dot!" Plunder managed the end of the thought before he too doubled over in glee.

Dropping the boy's hand, I rummaged in the pocket of my apron. I withdrew the crumpled paper that had traveled out of the Hall of Muses with us.

"This is what you are afraid of?" I held the paper high, so others could see

I unfolded the masterpiece with a flick of my wrist. The line of Trolls arched together into an interested and gawking crowd.

"What is that?" Some called out.

"Where did you make it?" Another question popcorned.

"That is the Dread Dot!" Burn stifled his giggles with a cough. He stood beside me.

"We . . ." Pillage jutted out her chin.

"Defeated it!" Plunder stood at attention.

The crowd stared wide-eyed. Disbelief flickered across their eyes. As if on cue, the doors at the top of the stairs clicked and swung open. All eyes shifted to the Muses standing in the open doors.

"Come in! Come in!" The Muses called out and waved the crowd in. "We moments ago finished settling the final pieces upon hook and pedestal. We hurried along when we heard the Queen herself would be joining us."

Astonished Trolls stared at the men and women in robes. Then, as if told there would be free candy, a flood of Trolls clattered and stomped up the stairs.

I clutched the Dread Dot to my chest and huddled together with Pillage, Plunder and Burn. We were still giggling as we tried not to be trampled by the sudden stampede.

Drake and the Queen came upon us in the surge. We slipped into line with them and climbed the stairs into the Hall of Muses.

The Muses had indeed made many changes since our last passage through the halls. The Trolls packed close together at first, though as their courage and awe washed out fear and unease, they milled through the galleries.

Shouts of, 'look, this one here is mine!' echoed as many of the Trolls picked out pieces they recalled creating so long ago.

My eyes swam, drinking in the colors and shapes gracing the walls. My muse, Carmen, met me with a smile that pronounced her cherubic cheeks. As we entered the main gallery, I was glad to be holding my muse's hand. We swept through the crowd, following the path we had created earlier in the journey. Carmen was yet another friend I had hardly gotten to know, and likely would not have proper chance to.

I nearly tumbled down the stairway while waving farewell to Carmen and the other muses.

"Whoa, now." Drake caught me and set me on my feet. "It would not do to be injured in a silly mishap after surviving so many epic battles."

"Yes!" Pillage and Plunder squealed in unison.

Burn sighed. "Are we nearly there?" He clapped his hands over his mouth.

"Burn!" A dozen boys scowled, before breaking into Puckish little grins.

"I didn't mean to say it." Burn fought to explain over the roar of laughter.

The Queen stepped off the last of the stone stairs. "We are here." She shook away a moment of sorrow traced over her face. A smile broke through as she led us forward to home.

The curve of the path ebbed into the hollow of a cavern mouth. Drake hung his head as he watched the Queen enter the opening. As she passed through the tunnel, a glow blossomed out around her. Her worn housemaid's dress melted away, becoming the flowing gowns she had first worn when I met her in the throne room. Drake's face pinched in a pained expression.

"What's wrong?" I asked.

Drake offered hardly a glance, a weak smile on his lips. He tousled my hair, but the familiar enthusiasm was not there. He walked on, feet dragging in the sand, seeming smaller than he had.

"He is not really a knight, Tierannie." Burn's eyes were solemn. "He is just a cook."

"But he is a hero." I choked back indignation on the giant's behalf.

Burn shrugged. He slumped his shoulders and marched along to catch up with Drake.

I scowled. My pace increased, as I moved through the tunnel filled with determination. Ignoring the confused looks as I marched past, I cut in front of the Queen.

"So, everything goes back to as it was before?" I crossed my arms in defiance and blocked her way.

"Tierannie." She had the humility to look ashamed. "These are the roles we play here."

"This is your world. You have magic, control of everything." My crossed arms shifted to hands clasped in plea.

The Queen sighed and looked over her shoulder at her waiting followers. "Some things cannot be changed with magic, no matter how much power one has."

"You are right." I grasped her hand and pulled her along the path.

The way branched at the end of the tunnel. It was clear by the glow on the left path that it led to the throne room. The smell of heat and a waft of oils, charcoal and food from the other, meant it led to the kitchen.

"Choose." I released the Queen's hand.

Her graceful shoulders slumped and she lowered her eyes. "Tierannie, someone must sit upon the throne or the kingdom will fall."

Recalling the fallen sky in the throne room when the Queen had been taken, I could not argue her point.

"Not all the time." I shook my head. "And not alone."

Drake and the Trolls caught up to us. They waited at the fork of the path, all eyes watching, attempting to understand what was happening.

The Queen's smile rose. She reached for Drake's hand. "Tierannie." You are like so many of your siblings, wise beyond years." Hand in hand, together, they followed the path toward the kitchen, where, for the next hour, the Queen and Drake moved over pots boiling over and food singing. It was all in the name of budding romance, so, even while Burn and his boys rolled their eyes at the behavior of their knight and mentor, not a single Troll complained as the smells wafting into the dining hall seemed a touch off from the norm.

The bell clanged from the archway of the kitchen. All attention turned to Drake and the Queen standing behind the table of bowls and the huge pot of food. Drake drew from his belt a serving ladle, and held it as a knight would a sword before leading a charge. He plunged the ladle into the large pot and began filling bowls. The Queen smiled at each of her Trolls as she served out the bowls heaped with food. When all were seated, she sat in an open place at the head of the long, narrow table.

Drake folded into a place beside her.

"Before we eat," the Queen announced, "a toast!" She raised her cup. "To my five champions, the destruction of the witch, the capture of the Dread Dot, and to properly welcome, Tierannie, the newest member of our family."

Cheers and cups rose toward the chandeliers. Trolls banged on tables until they rattled, and shook the room with stomping feet, in a gleeful earthquake. When the din calmed, we dove into our plates.

Slaying a witch did work up an appetite, though knowing this might be the last time in current company dimmed the flavor. I prodded bits of cake with the knob of a bare chicken bone, moving more food around the plate than into my mouth. As Trolls disappeared to homes and duties, the glory of the adventure ebbed away to expose the choice I would soon need to make.

While Drake and the Queen giggled over soap bubbles, I added my plate to those soaking in the sink. I joined in the cleaning, enjoying a moment to watch the love blossoming between the two, and stalling the inevitable conversation I would have to have with the Queen.

CHAPTER TWELVE:
HOME AGAIN AND GOING HOME

I assisted with the last of the dishes and Drake took his leave to prepare for the morning meal. I was alone with the Queen of the Trolls, at last.

"Your Majesty." I cleared my throat and choked back a sob, though I did not want to admit it.

The Queen smiled her radiantly down upon me. I thought about not being able to bask in that moon glow anymore, but thought too of the light and love that was Mother.

"I would like to go home." I straightened my shoulders and raised my head. "To my Up There home."

I had said the words. There was no taking it back now.

The Queen nodded knowingly. "I imagine that was a difficult choice to make."

I caught my cheeks in my palms and let the tears flow over my hands. It felt good to release all the feelings held back from the adventure. The Queen lifted my chin with a delicate hand. She gently wiped away my tears with the corner of her apron.

"I want you to be happy, Tierannie. That cannot be, while you still wonder about your Mother and Auntie."

The Queen's words were true. Through it all, no matter the terror, I had wondered and worried about Mother, and even about Auntie.

The Queen of the Trolls took my hand in hers. Side by side, we walked into the Jungle. We spoke of everything and nothing. By the time my head ducked under the opening to the Grotto, my deepest fears had melted away.

"Remember, Tierannie, Emily, you always have a home here." The Queen of the Trolls stepped back and raised her hands in a graceful wave. "You are a brave Troll and a wise young girl."

It was too late to change my mind. The world blurred and melted like a stream in a thaw. Colors shifted and ran in my vision.

"Emily!" Mother screamed in the distance.

I rubbed at my eyes and blinked at the rippling waves below. I dangled over the stream, the string still hanging from the bridge. The ribbon twisted. The spool slipped. I splashed into the cool water of the stream. The shallow, pebbled bed broke my fall. Murky water pooled around me and soaked my clothes clean through, but only bruises, nothing broken.

"Impressive dive, munchkin!" Trevor applauded from the shore.

Mother silenced him with a look darker than anything I had ever seen her give.

I sloshed out of the water into Mother's waiting

arms.

"What were you thinking?" She held me close in her soft embrace even as she scolded me. Pushing me to arms length Mother felt for broken or displaced bones. "You could have killed yourself."

Trevor smiled over Mother's shoulder. "Kid, you gave your mom, here, quite a scare." I sensed the concern in his tone, but his smile let me know everything would be okay.

He moved to the foot of the bridge and leaned to inspect the structure. "You know, I bet it wouldn't take much to repair this old bridge and make it a much safer place for Emily to play."

Mother shook her head but before her words could form, Auntie's voice cut through the air.

"Better to just tear it down!" The cruelty was clear in her voice.

The Grotto was my only thought as Auntie's cold words and colder stare touched me. I squished my dripping body and damp clothes against Mother's skirts. "Please! Please don't tear down the bridge! Please don't tear it down!"

Mother's face paled at my sudden display of emotion over a crumbling bridge. "Emily, Auntie is right. The bridge is dangerous. It should be repaired, but you know we don't have the time or money for such an undertaking."

Auntie had finally taken in the full scene. "Emily! Why are your clothes soaked again?" The old woman shuffled forward against her cane. "You are dripping on your shoes!"

I may have stood up to a dread Dot and helped to defeat an evil witch, but Auntie was another more menacing matter, altogether.

"Auntie, please. Emily was just playing and fell into the stream. I am certain she will not do it again." Mother's words fell weakly against the wall of Auntie's determination, but I thanked her silently for trying to cover for my mistake.

"Bah!" Auntie's gnarled fingers reached for my wrist. "That is like a whipping with a feather."

I pulled away from Auntie's reach and shifted to a safe distance behind Mother.

"Auntie, that's enough." I had never seen Mother stand up to the old woman with such strength.

I tucked my hands into my apron pockets, attempting to hide at least a small part of myself from Auntie's impending rush of anger. Within the folds of fabric the rattle bumped my knuckles. The marble slid within the rattle and pinged quietly against the bell. The whisper of a noise reminded me, I had stood up to a witch.

"Auntie, I know I owe you quite a lot, but I am no longer a child, and Emily is my responsibility." Mother stood between Auntie's cane and me.

I took hold of her hand and with the other I held the rattle in my apron pocket.

"Fine then!" Auntie shook her cane as her voice trembled in anger. "You have it your way, but in a few years, when she has gone wild, chasing boys and the like . . ." Her voice trailed off.

Looking past Mother, Auntie's eyes shifted to the stream and the hole in the bridge. Trevor, Mother and I followed the old woman's gaze to the gentle ripples of the water.

Trevor and Mother squinted, but I knew they did not see what I did.

A glow emanated from the water, but it came

from far below, in a place with more power than anything on the surface world.

The rattle continued to shiver in my apron pocket. I stepped around Mother to stand toe to toe with Auntie. Her growing scowl did not sway my courage. This confrontation was no different than facing down the Dot. This adversary was no different than the witch. I gripped the handle of the rattle as a knight might a sword.

My knuckles were surely white as I gripped the rattle for courage. "Why can't you just be nice?" The words did not come out in a yell, or a squeak. I breathed the phrase out slowly, as if invoking some power deep within the words. The energy of the rattle and all the Trolls coursed through my body up from the soles of my feet.

Auntie's jaw slacked open, her eyes wide with astonishment or perhaps confusion.

Mother's anger softened to concern. "Auntie? Are you okay?"

Trevor ran and grabbed a chair off the porch. He assisted Mother in resting Auntie into the seat. The old woman's eyes sparkled and danced. A dazed look trembled in her face. Then, she smiled.

Mother and Trevor sat on the grass in front of Auntie's chair. They looked to one another; shock and confusion passed between them. Auntie laughed. No, it was a giggle. She waved at me over Mother and Trevor's heads.

I squeezed the rattle as wonder and trepidation moved through my fingers. Was this another demonstration of the power of the key locked within the bell? After a time, Mother took Auntie's hands and helped her from the chair. The four of us walked up the hill to the house.

Shortly after a much-needed bath, I heard the door open downstairs and Mother welcomed in the doctor. Their voices traveling up the stairs from the sitting room were not clear enough to understand from my perch at the top of the landing. Not wanting to be discovered as I moved closer, I slipped along the wall. I wanted to hear the news about Auntie, without the adults filtering it for me.

Sounds of the doctor packing his travel bag carried around the corner along with the conversation. "She has shown signs in the past. You will have to keep a very close eye on her now." He paused a moment. "She does seem to be in a better mood than I have seen her."

I pressed against the wall as footsteps approach. None of the passing adults noticed me, their thoughts on more pressing matters.

"Thank you, Doctor." Mother saw him out.

Trevor lingered in the foyer, hands in his pockets. I remained as hidden as I could behind the curve of the banister.

"I am ashamed to admit this." Mother's eyes danced in the light as she gazed at Trevor. "I am relieved. I have never seen her so happy."

Trevor shifted his feet and cleared his throat. His hands were still in his pockets. "You are probably going to need a lot more help around here now."

"Yes." Mother nodded, her eyes wandering the room. "That is true."

"I . . . " Trevor's voice faltered. He cleared his throat and tried again. "I would like to be there for you."

Trevor's nervous swallow carried to my ears even

as far away as I sat. The note from the Hall of Muses appeared in my mind.

"I would like that very much." Mother's hands entwined with Trevor's as the two gazed at one another.

The step creaked as my weight shifted. Mother and Trevor both looked over at the sound. A sweet blush bloomed on their cheeks.

"It has been a very busy day, Emily." Mother little understood the depth of her own statement. "I think it is best if you go on to bed."

"I think so, too." I waved to Trevor and Mother before peering around the wall to wave to Auntie, who sat smiling by the fire. "Good night, Mother."

Dreams came quickly. Auntie's resting form appeared below me, as I floated through the quiet house. Her lips parted in a soft smile, but she did not wake. Hovering above the bed, I watched her sleep. She did not look like the same cold-hearted woman. In losing her mind, Auntie lost the weight of bitterness and years of hard memories that burdened her. I kissed her wrinkled cheek.

Down the staircase, around the entryway, through the short hall into the yard, I floated. In the twilight, I saw movement near the Temple of Venus. I swam through the air toward the rose-circled gazebo and settled onto the lawn.

Mother stood just outside the ring of rose bushes, a coffee colored shawl hugged to her shoulders. Trevor gently rocked each pillar, testing the stability of the structure. They paid no notice to me.

Trevor jumped from the platform avoiding the rotting steps. He embraced Mother and pressed his lips to hers. They both seemed to glow with joy.

A glinting near the bridge caught my attention, drawing me away from the romantic spectacle. My feet fleeted over green blades of grass. At the center of the bridge, I peered through the hole into the darkness below. A face glittered beneath the surface of the stream. The features obscured by the gentle ripple of water.

Astonishment pushed me to my feet.

The beautifully grotesque face rose from the stream. Water dripped from tendrils of pearls as the mask hovered before me at eye level. As the night air dried the crown of feathers, recognition dawned on me.

"Your purpose here has been fulfilled. It is time for you to leave. You are a Troll, Tierannie." As it spoke, the pearls across the forehead gently clacked, the fangs scraped lightly against the lower lip.

"I can't go back." The words stabbed at my soul. "The way is closed."

Tears welled against my lashes. The mask hovered closer still, but I did not back away. The water rippled. Three more masks floated up and out of the stream. Positioned in a triangle around my mask, the masks of Burn, Pillage and Plunder hovered.

"Why did you leave without saying goodbye?" They seemed to sag in the air.

"Why would you leave us at all?" Burn's mask asked.

"Don't you like us?" Pillage's mask tilted toward me.

"I do like you." I cried out. "And I want to go back. Mother and Trevor are happy together. Auntie is no longer mean and cold. They would be fine without me." My head hung as I fought to shake away my bubbling emotions. "Only, I don't know how to get back to the grotto."

I crumpled to my knees. Heaving sobs wracked my shoulders. Tears speckled the stone of the bridge. A chill rippled through my bare arms. My hands slid over the cool, smooth stones. "Stop trying to rationalize everything away." My mask spoke from above. "This is real. We are real. And, they have been watching you."

I rubbed my eyes wiping at the stream of tears. I followed the mask as it floated over my head. Standing at the edge of the water, Mother and Trevor stared at the floating masks, wonder in their eyes.

"Mother." I scrambled to my feet. "You can see them? You can see me?" The questions tumbled from my lips as I wiped at the tears on my cheeks.

"Emily." Mother pulled away from Trevor to kneel in front of me. "You found your real family."

I could not tell if her tears were joy or sorrow. I wrapped my arms around her shoulders. She hugged me back.

"Mother!" I sniffled back the tears. "I love you! You protected me from Auntie, and cared for me the best you could in this lonely old house. But I don't know where I belong."

The water shimmered in a vibrant blue glow, and the Queen of the Trolls emerged as if ascending a stairway. "We will take good care of her, as we would have taken care of you, had your father gone through with his sorrow driven plan to offer you to the river." The Queen stood over me as she spoke to

Mother.

I gazed into her beautiful emerald eyes.

The Queen turned her shimmering green eyes toward the house and raised a hand in a graceful wave that rippled the air with a charge of energy. In the distance, my bedroom window banged opened against the side of the house. The curtain whipped in the breeze, lapping at the edges of the frame. The rattle flew over the open yard, blowing the grass flat as it passed. The Queen caught the precious item in her hand. With a gentle gliding step, she moved toward me, and set the rattle in my palm. My fingers closed around the handle.

"You hold a key to the Kingdom of the Trolls, Tierannie. Be welcome, but know time is not as easy to manage up here." As gracefully as if she were descending a stair, the Queen of the Trolls disappeared below the surface of the water. The masks paraded behind their queen.

I kissed Mother's pale cheek. "Thank you for caring for me as Emily, but I have to go be Tierannie now. I will always remember what you did for me."

Trevor called from the shore. "Tierannie. I promise to fix your bridge for you."

I smiled, "And, you will take good care of Mother too. Yes."

He nodded, a faint blush tinting his cheeks. "Of course."

Mother blushed as well before slipping her hand into Trevor's.

I waved a final farewell to Mother and Trevor, from the top arch of the bridge. I pointed the rattle through the hole in the crumbling bridge. The water below swirled and funneled, forming a tube just wide enough for one small troll to slide through. I tucked the rattle into my sleeve and, with a shove, spiraled back into the Grotto—this time forever.

ABOUT THE AUTHOR

Born in small town Whitesboro, New York, J.J.M.Czep is the daughter of entrepreneurial parents. She spent much of her childhood wandering fields and swamplands surrounding her parents' home. Content to create imaginary companions and adventures, she took to writing down the stories in her overactive imagination. To become a better writer, she belly-dances, participates in rapier tournaments, and cavorts with pirates, mermaids, faeries, and mystics. She shares her peaceful home with her cats and teenage son.

www.jjmczep.com

ABOUT THE ILLUSTRATOR

Sarah Price is an honors graduate of Cazenovia College where she earned a BFA in Visual Communications with a Specialization in Advertising and Graphic Design. Sarah's art has received recognition at a number of juried exhibitions. Her preferred medium is digital illustration, in which the art begins as a sketch that is scanned, then rendered in Adobe Illustrator. Besides her artwork, Sarah enjoys playing piano, cooking, and reading. She resides in Whitesboro, NY with her husband Rob Meyer and their 2 cats. She is currently working on her first children's book.

http://www.artbysarahprice.com

Made in the USA
Columbia, SC
05 December 2024

47452001R00096